TWISTED
BONES

BOOKS BY HELEN PHIFER

HELEN PHIFER

TWISTED
BONES

bookouture

Published by Bookouture in 2025

An imprint of Storyfire Ltd.
Carmelite House
50 Victoria Embankment
London EC4Y 0DZ

www.bookouture.com

The authorised representative in the EEA is Hachette Ireland
8 Castlecourt Centre
Dublin 15 D15 XTP3
Ireland
(email: info@hbgi.ie)

ISBN: 978-1-83618-850-6
eBook ISBN: 978-1-83618-849-0

For Sam Thomas and Tina Sykes, my best friends, coffee gals and favourite fictional PCSOs. Thank you both, life would be dull without you in it. Xxx

ONE

BEFORE

Martha MacKay had spent an hour in the church huddled up on the pew nearest the radiator that gave off the most heat. There were many other pews in the huge space, but she knew this one gave off the hottest air, having spent so many nights here sheltering from the cold. It was a prime spot, often sought out by the other street girls or homeless people who spent the night in Bridge Street Church to stop them freezing to death out in the bitter winter. Thank God in more ways than one for the sanctuary this place offered.

Martha wasn't a religious woman; her parents had never gone to a church except for the usual weddings, christenings and funerals. She had been brought up with a loathing of God that she never understood until she was old enough to realise her parents blamed any misfortune on themselves and the world at God's feet. Martha, though she was savvy enough to thank the good Lord when any good fortune came her way, didn't hold the same amount of bitterness towards Him that her mum and dad had. This place was the closest thing to home she had now; her parents had both disowned her and then her dad had dropped down dead one day, and she'd never even got to say goodbye. Here, there were always kind people around, always ready to dish out food, second-hand clothes and advice, not that she ever listened to it. Her dad always said she was too stubborn for her own good and look at the state she was in now. She had the use of a one-bedroom flat she could go to if the other girls weren't using it. Four of them shared that hovel but lately it was too much for her to stand. The pungent odour of alcohol and sex lingered in the air like the world's worst plug-in air freshener. Martha didn't want to live that way. She'd had enough of giving herself to men who thought nothing of trying to choke her, hit her, slap her – all to get their rocks off for twenty quid. She wanted a life, her own flat that smelled so much better; she wanted to live a life where she didn't have to rely on the charity of a church to keep her going.

'Martha, how are you this evening?'

The warm, soothing tones of the vicar's voice was like sucking on a honey and lemon throat lozenge, the kind her dad always had in his pocket and offered up whenever she had a cough or runny nose. Tonight, she was missing him more than she'd thought was possible. 'I'm cold, but I'm alive.'

Theo laughed. 'Alive is always good. Why don't you go get a sleeping bag out of the cupboard and get snuggled down in it, before they all go walkabout. We had a fresh delivery of them off the council this morning.'

'I already had one this month.' She didn't know what it was about this particular vicar, but lying to him was out of the question, she couldn't do it. His face was so kind, his manner so nice, he would be a perfect husband to someone, and it made her sad that it would never, ever in a million years be her. She heard the whispers that he preferred men to women, though it didn't matter to her if he preferred dinosaurs, she just wished it could be different. Not that he'd look at her and find her attractive because she knew she wasn't. It was nice to dream though, dreams were all she had.

'Well, I won't tell if you don't. Have you eaten tonight, had a hot drink?'

She shook her head, too scared to move and lose her prime spot. As if sensing this, Theo smiled at her. 'Leave it with me, I'll be back soon.'

He walked away, and she felt her cheeks begin to burn and her eyes begin to blur. She was being right soppy tonight, it was stupid. Maybe it was the stonking great Christmas tree in the corner a few rows in front of her, its sparkling fairy lights bringing back all the painful memories she tried so hard to forget about her life before her dad had died. After he was gone was a painful, ugly mess, and she didn't care about that too much. She just wished she could see him again and tell him how much she loved him, what a great dad he was and how her mum was a mess who had never deserved him in the first place. She hadn't known she was crying until the tree lights began to blur.

'Here you are. Why are you so upset tonight? It's not like you.'

Theo was next to her, crouching down offering her a mug of hot chocolate and half a packet of digestive biscuits. She took them from him, her icy fingertips brushing against his warm ones. 'Thank you.'

He shrugged. 'My pleasure, the soup has all gone but I've asked John to make you a sandwich and I'm going to get you a sleeping bag. I was supposed to be kicking everyone out tonight, but it's too cold out there, and what is a house of God without its people?' He winked at her and straightened, striding off to the store cupboard where the blankets and sleeping bags were kept.

He returned minutes later with a rolled-up blue bag and a blanket. 'You'll not freeze on my watch, Martha; do you need to talk about anything?'

She shook her head. 'I'm good, thank you, just feeling a little bit sorry for myself.'

He reached out and gently touched her shoulder. 'I'm around if you need anything. John should be here soon with your sandwich.'

She clutched the sleeping bag to her chest and wrapped the blanket around her shoulders. If she had some money she could get away from this life. She'd run away once and ended up here, but what would it be like to run away with a pocket full of cash?

'There you go.'

There was a guy she knew of, but didn't know by name. He'd been around longer than Theo and was standing in front of her holding a plate of sandwiches; they were cut into small triangles like her dad used to cut them.

'Thank you.'

'What's up with your face? You look miserable.'

This man wasn't the same as Theo. There was a hardness behind those small black eyes that were too narrow for his round face.

'Nothing.'

'Are you not working tonight?' He grinned at her, and she felt her skin crawl.

'No, it's too cold. There's no one out there.'

He put his hand in his trouser pocket and pulled out a wad of twenty-pound notes, so many she felt her eyes bulge out of her head.

'I could pay you.'

'What for?'

'To show me a good time. Isn't that what you do?'

Martha needed cash, and that was a lot of money, but she had some morals. 'I'll not give you a blow job in a church.'

He began to laugh. 'For this amount of cash, I'd want a lot more than a blow job and I wouldn't expect you to do it in here.

Why don't we go to the canal, no one will be down there now, and you can show me just how much you'd like this money.'

She shook her head. It was bloody freezing outside, and there was a good chance she'd die of hypothermia before she'd even finished what she started. As he walked away, she wondered if she should. Did she need the money this much? The answer as always was yes, she needed his cash. Finishing her sandwich, she stashed the sleeping bag and blanket under the wooden pew so nobody else could steal it.

Martha stepped out from the warmth of the church into an icy darkness, so still she felt the coldness seep deep into her bones. She paused in the shadow of the church, his presence behind her, wondering if this was going to be worth it, then hurried across the road to the towpath alongside the canal where the streetlights didn't work and the biting wind that blew across the water made her entire body shudder.

TWO

Ettie had woken early, too early, at the sound of Max, her pet raven, tapping on her window. Well, he wasn't her pet as such, she hadn't bought him from a shop or person, and she didn't own him – she never could, or would want to. Max was quite the independent bird who came and went as he pleased. Ettie liked to think that it was the opposite way around; she was Max's pet. Either way it didn't matter, the bird was excellent company, and she adored him, not to mention they shared a love of warm, buttery, freshly baked shortbread biscuits that they would often bond over.

When she'd opened her window to greet him good morning, he had a sprig of fresh pine in his beak that he dropped onto the sill before beginning to preen himself. It had smelled so wonderful and reminded her she needed to get making her Christmas candles for the farmers' market or they wouldn't be cured in time. Max often brought her presents and she treasured every single one, but this time it was as if he had read her mind and knew she needed a little push in the right direction. The last few weeks she had been a bit lost if she was honest. She missed Morgan, who she hadn't seen for a while, and she hated to bother her when she was always so busy at work.

Ettie had been making candles by hand since she could remember. It was her favourite out of all the crafty things she did by far. She loved picking herbs, drying them and using them for her special blends of teas too, but there was something so satisfying about making your own candles. Working diligently in her kitchen that really was the heart of her home, she carefully measured out the wax then put it in a large Pyrex jug to slowly melt on the electric hotplate she kept especially for this purpose. In the beginning she'd been a stickler for testing the temperature with a cooking thermometer, but now she relied on her instinct to know when the wax was hot enough. Then she set about choosing the essential oil blends to go into the hot wax when it reached the right temperature. Pine, cedar, eucalyptus and cranberry for a wintery smelling batch. Orange, clove, cinnamon for a more traditional yule smelling batch. Ettie had already dried a tray of fresh orange slices in the oven and had some cranberries to use to decorate the candles, but she needed some more sprigs of fresh pine.

Once she had poured the wax into the beautiful cut-glass containers she collected from the assorted charity and vintage shops she loved to browse in around the Lakeland villages and towns, she would go for a walk in the woods to collect the pine.

The radio newscaster told her there was a chance of more snow in the next couple of hours. Ettie loved the snow; well, at her age she enjoyed staring at it from her cottage window with a roaring fire in the hearth and a mug of coffee in her hand. She didn't enjoy trudging through it so much, though the ground was just about walkable at the moment. There was a thin coating of snow but if she wore her heavy boots, she would be okay. She was tempted to leave it, but the sprigs of pine would look so pretty on the candles; it was the little finishing touches that seemed to make them more attractive to her customers.

Ettie knew it was now or never; if the snow came there was no telling how long it could last.

Taking her wicker basket and a pair of pruning shears, she wrapped up well; thermal underwear, thick jumper, cardigan, scarf, hat, gloves, two pairs of thick socks and her trusty bird flying above her head, leading her to the riverbank where the most beautiful pine trees grew.

There was something satisfying about listening to the crunch of her boots on the crisp ground. The woods were too quiet today, no birdsong, no people, it was a little eerie, but it didn't bother Ettie. She had lived in these woods for over thirty years, and she was used to it.

As she veered off the path and cut through the trees, she heard the rushing of the river as it gurgled through the woods. Ettie's eyes fell on the bleached-white slender fingers of what looked like a hand reaching out of the water, as if it was trying to catch her attention, and she shook her head. There was no way a hand could be sticking out of the water like that, it must be a fallen branch. She blinked and walked a little nearer to the river's edge. Gasping, she cupped a hand across her mouth in both shock and fear.

She wasn't wrong – it was a hand. Only, the flesh had been stripped from the fingers. She was staring at the skeletal bones of what had once been someone's hand. It was attached to an arm that still had flesh on it, and Ettie stared at the small faded rose tattoo on the wrist, trying to figure out what exactly she was staring at. It was then she realised that the rest of the body was just below the surface, the clothing ballooning and waving around as if it was still moving.

There was no way Ettie could get to whoever it was to help them, as they were caught on a tree that had fallen partway across the river, so she turned and began hurrying back to her cottage to get help, Max soaring above her, cawing loudly as they returned home.

THREE

Detective Constable Morgan Brookes was blissfully happy. The spa afternoon that Ben had bought her for her birthday had turned out to be the best present she'd been given in a long time. The masseuse was doing an amazing job of kneading all the knots between her shoulder blades. She had invited Wendy along because Ben had told her he'd rather poke himself in the eye with a stick than spend an afternoon with a load of semi-naked women in hot tubs, guzzling Prosecco and screeching like hyenas.

She opened one eye and looked through the gap in the blinds. Oh how wrong he'd been on that level – there was only Wendy out there and they had the place to themselves. She closed her eyes again as the hot stones were laid on her back and had to stop herself from sighing. The rumble of her phone in the pocket of the white fluffy dressing gown hanging off the peg by the door broke her moment of bliss. She glanced at the masseuse, who was frowning.

She wasn't on call; it was her afternoon off. She had put in a rest day in lieu of the hundreds she'd accumulated. She'd finished work just two hours ago. Only Ben or work phoned her, and she knew it wouldn't be Ben, as he had been adamant that she leave her phone in the car whilst she was in the spa. But she liked to read books on it and after her massage she was planning on lying on a waterbed to read. Wendy sometimes called her; she was probably the closest friend she had out of work. Declan rang on the rare occasion.

She opened one eye again to see Wendy standing up now, on her phone, and she knew by her stance something was wrong. *Fuck*, she whispered to herself. Opening both eyes she watched as Wendy began walking towards her. She pushed herself up onto her elbows and the stones slid from her back and clattered to the tiled floor. As Wendy knocked on the door of her small room, the masseuse turned at the loud noise, glaring at Morgan's lack of respect and relaxation plus the fact that the scattered stones were on the floor.

'Morgan, are you decent?'

'Sort of, what's up?'

Wendy opened the door wide, the masseuse was picking up the stones.

'Sorry about that, could you give us a minute, please?'

The masseuse was still glaring at the pair of them before forcing a smile on her face. She nodded curtly and walked out.

Wendy walked in.

'Your aunt Ettie.'

Morgan gasped, not wanting to know what she was about to say next.

'She's fine, sorry, I should have worded that better. Well, she's not that fine, she's found a body in the river near her cottage. Ben said not to disturb you, but Joe has gone to help the Barrow CSI document a cannabis factory in a disused takeaway building, so I need to go and I couldn't just walk out and leave you without telling you where I was going.'

Morgan pulled the blanket around her and clambered off the bed. 'I can't exactly lie here whilst you're dealing with that.

I need to make sure Ettie is okay. She's all the family I have. Give me a minute.'

Wendy grimaced. 'Ben will kill me for this, I shouldn't have told you.'

'Ben can sod off. What did he think would happen? That I'd not wonder where you'd gone, if you'd got up and walked out leaving me here on my own.'

A raucous group of women all laughing loudly walked past the open door to Morgan's room, glasses of Prosecco in hands, breaking the peace and tranquillity. Morgan thought maybe Ben did have a point. She turned to watch them as she said to Wendy, 'It's not like I can relax now, is it? I'm coming with you. And anyway, you gave me a lift here. It's too far to walk back. You can't leave me stranded in the middle of the Langdales.'

Wendy shrugged. 'I'll wait for you in the changing rooms.'

She closed the door, and Morgan pulled the dressing gown on. Pulling her phone out of her pocket she saw she had two missed calls from Ettie's number on the screen, and dialled her straight back. It went to voicemail. Damn, she'd not even heard the previous call. She rang again but heard the automated message and hung up. Desperate to get to her aunt she rushed out of the room. The beauty therapist was standing there with her arms crossed.

'Thank you, that was amazing, but I have to go, there's a family emergency.'

At this the woman's eyes softened. 'Sorry to hear that, I hope everything is okay.'

Morgan smiled at her and thought, *so do I.*

The small car park that led through Covel Woods, where Ettie's cottage was nestled amongst the trees, was full of police vehicles. Luckily for them no walkers had been parked up, making it easier to close off the scene. Blue-and-white police tape had been tied around the entrance and an officer was standing in front of it. Neither Morgan nor Wendy recognised her, but she clearly knew them as she waved them forwards and lifted the tape so Wendy could drive under it. They waved back, and she smiled.

As they got out of the car, Wendy muttered, 'Bloody hell, I'm a total idiot.'

'What's up?'

'I'm in my own car; I forgot to go get the CSI van. That's so stupid, what was I thinking?'

'Have you not got anything in the boot?'

She arched one eyebrow at Morgan. 'No, unlike you and Ben, I don't carry around a full forensic kit and protective clothing. I have a life outside of work. Some of us don't want to be on call twenty-four seven.'

Morgan arched an eyebrow at her. 'Really, then why are you here instead of getting your hot stone massage on your afternoon off?'

A smile appeared on Wendy's face so big it made her eyes sparkle, and all the annoyance dissipated. 'Bugger off, Morgan, it's your fault. You are a bad influence, that's why.'

'Whoa, did they downgrade the van, Wendy? Did you not tell them those kind of budget cuts are too far?' Cain's voice echoed out of the clearing to the trees. Wendy, who was already out of the car, headed towards Cain whilst Morgan pulled down the sun visor to check her appearance. She felt sick; she'd taken her eyeliner and make-up off before going into the spa and it made her feel like the gangly teenage girl who had been sad and lonely. Her eyeliner was like her body armour, but it was too late now, she needed to go see her aunt and make sure she was okay.

She got out and headed towards the entrance to the woods where Cain and Wendy were in deep discussion. Head down she hurried past Cain before he could say anything and got past him to hear: 'Hello to you again, you just couldn't keep away. What's it been, like, two hours?'

'Hi, Cain.'

She carried on walking briskly to get to Ettie's cottage, which was only five minutes away when you knew the way to go. Max had shown her the right paths to use. She looked up for him; he was usually around. As she hit the small clearing which led to her aunt's cottage, she saw the purple front door was ajar and Max was perched on the matching purple gate like a gate-keeper, which she supposed he was. He looked after her aunt as good as any dog could.

'Hey, Max, what's going on?'

The bird cawed at her. He didn't take off as she reached the gate, instead he let her stroke his head before soaring into the sky. Morgan envied him a little that he could take off whenever he wanted.

'Morgan.'

Her aunt's voice sounded a lot quieter than it usually did, and Morgan turned to see her standing at her front door, face pinched and much paler than usual. Ettie had the most beautiful rosy cheeks, but there was no sign of them today, and her beautiful grey hair that was always kept in an immaculate bun had come loose and strands of it hung down her back and shoulders. A couple of strides and she was in her aunt's warm embrace, her arms tightly wrapped around her, squeezing and rocking from side to side, and it felt so good.

'Are you okay?'

Ettie nodded. 'It was a bit of a shock; I wasn't expecting it. I don't suppose anyone who finds a person like that ever does though.'

Ettie led Morgan inside and closed the door. The small, cluttered, homely cottage smelled of pine and eucalyptus. There was an assortment of beautiful cut-glass dishes on the kitchen side all with wicks in them. Some of them had creamy wax that was setting inside.

'Ettie, they are beautiful. I didn't know you could make candles.'

'Easiest thing in the world, Morgan, and such a lovely, therapeutic hobby too. I will show you how to do it one day, you will love it. I use all natural ingredients too: soy wax, my own essential oils made from the pines in the forest and the herbs from my garden. I thought I might give some as gifts and sell some at the farmers markets in the run up to Christmas. They need a few weeks to cure before they can be lit and will burn well. I realised it would be lovely to pick some sprigs of fresh pine to garnish the top of them and was happily wandering through the forest. The best pine trees are nearest the river, you see, so I headed in that direction and got the shock of my life when I saw her.' Ettie paused, swallowing a lump in her throat. 'She was caught up in some branches in the river, her clothes had snagged on them, I don't know how long she's been in there but—'

Morgan didn't rush her aunt, she guided her to the armchair she favoured and helped her to sit down. 'Let me make us some tea. Which do you think is best?'

Ettie smiled. 'I think a pot of M&S gold blend will do nicely with a drop of brandy in it. I'm not sure brandy and chamomile are a good mix.'

Morgan laughed. 'You're the expert, I'll do whatever you want.'

She busied making the tea. She would go and find Ben eventually, but right now her aunt needed her more than he did. He had Cain. Amy was around too because she'd declared a couple of weeks ago that she was no longer staying in the office and was doing what she'd always done. Nobody had argued with her, nobody dared to – her mood swings were off the scale now she was pregnant. She passed her aunt a cup of tea and found the bottle of brandy she kept in the back of her cupboard for emergencies. When she finally sat down opposite her, Ettie asked, 'Are you feeling well in yourself, Morgan? You look very fresh-faced and radiant, but I don't think I have ever seen you without your eyeliner, and before you get all self-conscious' – Ettie held up her hand – 'I want you to know that you look beautiful with or without it, I'm not passing judgement.'

Morgan laughed. 'I'm very well, I was in the middle of a hot stone massage when I was told what had happened.'

'Oh, dear Lord. Your one chance to have some you time and I go and spoil it by finding a dead body. I am so sorry.'

Morgan reached out and squeezed her aunt's hand. 'It's not your fault, I'm sorry you had to be the one to find it. Do you want to finish what you were telling me before?'

'She was, oh how do I put this without sounding crass? She had been there some time I think, although I'm not the expert here, but some of her fingers were only bones.'

Morgan wondered how this had happened. There were no local current missing persons cases that she was aware of. It had to be someone from out of the area, unless it was someone who had no one to report her as missing. She thought back to the body they had discovered in Whinlatter Forest a few years ago: Anna. No one had reported her missing either; it was all so sad and made her realise that not everyone had a family support network. If she wasn't with Ben, and hadn't discovered her aunt Ettie, Morgan would have been all alone too.

A loud knock on the door made them both start, Morgan almost spilling hot tea all over the place. She stood up, but before she could open the door she heard Ben's voice.

'Ettie, it's me, should I come in?'

'Yes, the door's unlocked.'

He walked in and did a double take to see Morgan standing there. 'Why are you here, Morgan?'

'Why wouldn't I be?'

He didn't say anything else, but she could tell he was annoyed she was here when she should be at the spa.

Ettie shrugged. 'It's my fault, I phoned Morgan before I rang the police. I was panicking and wasn't thinking straight.'

'That's okay, Ettie, you did the right thing. I am the police; I want to be here,' Morgan reassured her.

Ben's shoulders sagged a little, and Morgan scrutinised his face. He looked tired and stressed. He also looked as if he needed a spa day more than she did; he hadn't shaved this morning and his five o'clock shadow looked more like he was growing a beard. She worried about him, the pressure he was constantly under, the stress of the cases that never seemed to let up and give him a break. She pointed to the sofa. 'Sit, I'll make you a coffee and you can take five minutes.'

He did as he was told and she made him a mug of coffee, piping hot just the way he liked it. She sat next to him, and he took the mug from her and smiled. 'Thank you.'

Ettie shook her head. 'You know this would be such a lovely moment if the two of you were here for a visit that didn't involve your work.'

Ben grinned at her. 'I agree, we always mean to come visit, don't we, Morgan, but work doesn't seem to give us much of a break. How was your massage?'

'The part of it I had was wonderful. Next time, you're coming too. You look rough, Ben, you need to do something to destress.'

'Thanks, says the woman who dared to come out in public with no eyeliner.'

Her jaw slackened and she playfully punched him in the arm.

'Ouch, that's assault.'

Ettie smiled at him. 'You deserved it.'

'Oh, I see how it is. The two of you are ganging up on me, right.'

'No, dear. We are telling you because we both love you and care for you.'

He sighed and took a sip of the coffee. 'I'm a lucky guy.'

'Yes, you are, Ben.' Ettie winked at him.

He straightened his back and took out his beaten old notebook that had curling edges and pen scribbles all over the cover. 'Ettie, are you okay to answer some questions?'

'Of course, I'm tougher than I look, you should know that, Ben.'

'Good that's great, can you tell me exactly what you were doing when you saw the body? How you discovered it?'

'I was telling Morgan before you knocked on the door, I was looking for some fresh pine branches and the best trees grow near to the river, and I was down there when it caught my eye. Poor woman, I'm assuming it's a woman, I saw the fingers and I kind of rushed back to phone for help.'

Ben nodded. 'We think so.'

'Well, as you know, these woods are like my back garden. I've lived here a very long time and I can usually tell if there is something out of tune with the whole ambience, if there is something off-kilter, but it took me by complete surprise. I hadn't the slightest inkling there was something so terribly wrong. How long has she been there?'

'It's hard to say, that's not my area but I think quite some time.'

'She's been stuck in the river on that fallen tree all this time, she can't have been.'

'Why?'

'Well for one thing, the tree only fell a few weeks ago when we had that terrible storm, and it felt like it wasn't going to stop raining. She wasn't there then. And these woods are, unfortunately for me, a more popular spot for walkers than they've ever been. Somebody would have seen and reported her, surely.'

Morgan cringed, feeling bad for Ettie as there had been a lot of social media publicity about this area, due to the crimes that had happened recently, and then there was the capture of Johnson Stone who had held Ettie hostage inside her own home. Ettie didn't read the papers or use social media much, but it had been everywhere and no matter where you lived in the world, if a crime had happened, you could guarantee there would be people who'd want to come and look at the place for themselves. Morbid curiosity was a part of people's natures, how else would you explain why so many people turned up to watch public executions throughout history? Morgan felt a cold chill across the back of her shoulders, imagining standing for hours in a place where someone was going to lose their head to a guillotine or have a hangman's noose around their neck. She realised both Ben and Ettie were silent, both watching her.

'Sorry, just thinking. So, you don't think she could have been in the water more than a few weeks?'

Ettie shrugged. 'I'm no expert, dear, your friend will be able to tell you more, won't he? How is he doing, he's a fine specimen of a man if ever there was one.'

Morgan couldn't stop the grin that spread across her lips and knew exactly who her aunt was talking about. 'Oh, yes, he is. Declan's doing okay considering his partner was seriously injured not that long ago.'

'I read about that; poor guy, how is he doing?'

'As good as someone who was attacked with an ice axe can do I suppose.'

Ettie scowled at her. 'Is that good, bad, is he brain damaged or is he okay with regards to that?'

'He's struggling a bit; his memory isn't too good but I'm sure with time it will all come back to him.'

Ettie stood up and went to the dresser where she kept her jars of teas, and after debating over a couple of them she returned with one and passed it to Morgan.

'Please give him that, it's my very special healing tea. It will help him when he's having a hard day. It's full of soothing and medicinal herbs. He'll need a dollop of honey to help it go down though, it's slightly bitter but it's very good.'

Morgan smiled at Ettie. 'I could do with some of this too.'

'Then you shall have a jar, dear. To be honest I made it for you, but I haven't seen you to give it to you. How is your head now?'

'Much better and thankfully it wasn't as serious as Theo's.'

Ben was examining the glass jar containing the tea. 'What's in it?'

Morgan knew he was wary of Ettie's teas after some had been tampered with and used to poison and kill some women a couple of years ago.

'Nothing dangerous, Ben. Lavender, feverfew, chamomile and a few secret ingredients that are all perfectly safe to ingest.'

He nodded. 'That's good.'

Ettie rolled her eyes at him, making Morgan smile.

'Did you recognise the woman in the water, Ettie?' he asked.

She picked up her teacup and paused before answering. 'I don't think even if I'd stared at her for an hour that I would have recognised her, Ben.'

Ben's cheeks turned a fiery red, and Ettie leaned across and patted his knee. 'I'm teasing you, Ben, and I'm sorry because there is nothing funny about this and that poor woman' – her voice caught in the back of her throat, and she whispered – 'deserves more respect. No, I do not know her.'

Morgan felt her shoulders relax a little, feeling better that there was no connection to her aunt other than the body being dumped in the river close to her cottage.

Ettie straightened up. 'Will you be able to tell where she went into the water? She might have been washed downriver and getting caught in that tree stopped her from going any further.'

'Yes, we should be able to.'

Ben sounded hopeful, but Morgan wasn't so sure they could, as it all depended on if there were any forensics left. Of course, they would have search teams on either side of the river looking for a point of entry, but it could be a mammoth task and take some time, if they could find anything at all. The flurries of snow were getting thicker and the ground was coated in a fine layer.

FOUR

Theo was curled up on the armchair that Declan had dragged over to the bedroom window so he could watch the world going on from the safety of his bedroom. Wrapped in a heated throw with a book next to him that Morgan had dropped off and radio Cumbria playing in the background, he hadn't the heart to tell Declan that he couldn't concentrate on reading and instead was literally watching the clouds in the sky for the most part of the day. The snow had been a welcome distraction, and he had enjoyed watching the snowflakes falling against the glass, their beautiful patterns sticking to it. Father Gordon was doing a great job of covering for him at the church, and he knew that at some point he was going to have to go back in there, but at the moment he just couldn't face it. His brush with death had shaken him to his core. It wasn't something he'd ever thought about before, his own mortality. His left hand trembled when he held it in front of his face. He hadn't told Declan about that either. It was embarrassing enough that he was in this state and being looked after.

He had developed a newfound respect for Morgan. She had been injured in her work many times and yet she still went back to it, regardless of what she had been through. Here he was hiding away in his bedroom like some teenage drama queen, and he was mortified but unable to do anything to drag himself out of the depression he was sinking deeper into each day.

His phone vibrated on the windowsill, and he picked it up to see a message from an unknown number. Debating on whether to open it, his curiosity got the better of him.

Hey Theo, it's John. I used to help out at Bridge Street Church. Heard you got into a spot of bother and wondered if I could call in to see you tomorrow when I'm down that way? Be great to catch up.

Theo closed his eyes. John, John, how many Johns did he know that went to Bridge Street Church? He counted six on his fingers. Too polite to ask which John it was, he texted back.

Hi John, yes be good to see you. Do you know where to find me? St Martha's, Rydal Falls?

John sent him a thumbs up, and Theo put his phone down, no idea which John it was but he thought it might be nice to have a catch-up and talk about something other than his attack or what's on the television.

Movement across the front of the church caught his eye. It was Gordon. He had been accosted by Mrs Decker, who seemed to be having an animated conversation with him about something, and he hoped it wasn't anything to do with sorting out the photos for the calendar for next year. Maybe Theo's depression was God's way of getting him out of having to have that conversation himself. Nevertheless, he felt a little bad for Gordon, but not bad enough to consider going back to work before the final photos had been chosen. He shuddered, as kind as it was of them to do this, he was sure there were alternative ways to raise cash for the repairs to the roof. Gordon managed to extricate himself from Mrs Decker's iron-clad grip, and Theo smiled. They went back a long time, he and Gordon, working together in Theo's early days he was a very good mentor; for a moment he was lost inside his head, back in the busy inner-city church he had such fond memories of.

He heard Declan's Audi before he saw it and snapped himself out of the daydream he was in, and picking up the book, he began to read the first page it opened on, the words blurring and all merging into one. Maybe he should come clean and tell Declan he was struggling to concentrate, that reading was out of the question. He watched Declan jump out of the car and dash towards the front door, and his heart swelled with the love he felt for the clever, handsome guy who just happened to be the love of his life.

'Theo?'

'Upstairs.'

Declan's boots thudded up the stairs and he burst into the room like an excited child. Rushing towards him he bent down and kissed his forehead.

'How are you?'

Theo shrugged. 'Bored.'

'Bored enough to start work?'

'Erm, not that bored. Why are you here in the middle of the day?'

'I thought I should be the one to tell you, before you read it on social media.'

'Tell me what?'

'A body has been found in the river, in Covel Woods, and it's suspicious. I'm on my way there to assess it.'

Declan was watching his face for any sign of distress. Theo pushed himself up, so he was standing facing him. He was an inch shorter than his partner. Putting his hands on Declan's shoulders he smiled. 'I'm good, I'm not locked away in here because I'm scared of being attacked again. I'm hiding in here because I'm scared of Mrs Decker and her gang.'

Declan grinned at him and laughed so loud it made Theo jump. 'For the love of God, is she still wanting to run around with her baps out?'

Theo nodded. 'It would seem so, Gordon said he doesn't know what to do with her, she's on a mission.'

'A mission from God?' Declan asked.

Theo shook his head, giving himself a headache. 'The good Lord may work in mysterious ways, but I'm pretty sure even He would draw the line at Mrs Decker's baps.'

The pair of them collapsed onto the end of the bed, laughing hard. Declan pulled Theo close, holding him. 'Well, as long as you're okay with it. I'm afraid living around here is never going to ease the painful memories for you. There is too much violent death for a place as beautiful on the outside as it looks.'

'The most beautiful of souls can hide the darkest of secrets.'

Declan studied his face. 'Is that some kind of confession? If it is you're talking to the wrong guy, but I do know this handsome priest who can help you out when he decides to get himself out of this room and go back to doing what he loves.'

'You do, huh?'

'Oh, yes. He's a dream.'

Theo didn't think his heart could swell any bigger than it already was, it was fit to burst.

'Well, that's just as well. Maybe you could put me in touch with him.'

'I'll pass your name on.' Declan winked at him, kissed him briefly then stood up. 'For a man of God, you are a bad influence on me. I almost forgot I'm on duty and on my way to a crime scene.'

Theo sat up and smiled at him. 'Would that be such a bad thing? Nobody should have to deal with the number of deaths you do.'

Declan tilted his head, then threw it back and roared with laughter. 'This priest I know, he's also a comedian. I hate to break this to you, but my entire job revolves around dead people, it's what I do. Day in, day out, I help the dead to hopefully find peace in the next life or wherever they go. I'm their voice, I can help their loved ones to cope by telling them what happened to the most important person in their world. I'm just glad I didn't have to do the same for you.'

Theo smiled. 'Yeah, me too, me too. Be safe, I suppose Morgan is already at the scene. She's as bad as you are. If you see her tell her this book is pants and has she got anything with a gruesome murder in it.'

Declan's eyes widened. 'You want to read about murder after what happened? I told her to give you something motivational, not gory.'

'Ah, so this is your fault. Yes, I'd rather have a brutal murder, something that makes me think I got off lightly will do.'

'Noted, I will tell her. I don't know when I'll be back.'

Theo shrugged. 'That's okay, I'll be here. I love you, be careful.'

Declan was already walking back down the stairs. 'I love you too, and I always am.'

Theo turned back to the window to watch the love of his life driving away, a part of him feeling guilty as he pushed the memories back down that were threatening to explode. Everyone had dark secrets, even men of God.

FIVE

Ben led Morgan to where the mountain rescue team and the fire service were in the process of recovering the body. The river was fast flowing with all of the recent rainfall and the snowy banks were making it more difficult for them. She felt a wave of sadness for the woman who had been washed downstream and had spent her last days in the icy-cold churning waters of the river. Her body being there didn't necessarily mean she had been murdered, she could have fallen in and drowned, not been able to get back out. There had been a tragic case not that long ago, when the Cumbrian dog section had been involved in the search of Nicola Bulley, whom people suspected had been murdered but had drowned accidentally; this was Rydal Falls though, and inside of Morgan's gut was that niggly, churning feeling that told her this was probably no accident. She stared at the woman's face, her eyes following down her body to an arm that was caught in the deadwood of the fallen tree and then down to her fingers of which some were partly skeletal. She felt herself transported back into the past, to Anna, whose body had been in the forest a long time. Nobody had realised she was missing, and she wondered if Anna's ghost was telling her something of the similarities. But the guy who had murdered her, Miles Gilbert, was inside prison.

Glancing at Ben, he nodded. 'First impressions?'

'I think this is more than a simple drowning.'

'Why?'

'Her fingers, Ben, they're skeletal. The question is, where did she come from, where has she been before ending up in there, and why is the skin missing from her hand? We have no female, long-term missing persons on our system. How long has she been dead?'

He shrugged. 'I wish I knew.'

Morgan walked as close to the riverbank as she could so as not to interfere with the rescue crews who were working diligently to recover her. There were four fire and rescue guys alongside three mountain rescue workers, two were in the water and two were on the riverbank. The rest of the fire crew were standing away from the scene watching their colleagues. Morgan could see the woman's bleached blonde hair had a thick band of dark roots at the crown, not the kind you get when you go to the hairdressers for a balayage. It was a home bleaching job and reminded her of her own mum Sylvia's hair. She used to bleach it at home then put a rinse over the top of it so it was a purple-platinum colour – that was before purple shampoo became a thing in their house. Sylvia hadn't bothered with her hair in the days before her suicide though, she hadn't bothered with a lot of things; there had been signs something was wrong, but Morgan was a teenage girl then, full of her own angst and problems. She hadn't really paid much attention to Sylvia's downward spiral into the blackness she hadn't been able to escape from, much to her own regret. Even Stan hadn't noticed, and he should have, he was her husband. Morgan's heart ached for Sylvia; she had desperately needed help but no one had been there to give it.

Several loud shouts and lots of splashing snapped her back

to the present. They had managed to untangle the body, but one of the fire crew had lost his footing on the slimy riverbed and slipped, going under the fast-flowing water and letting go. The rope around the woman's waist had slithered off like a coiled snake and she'd begun floating away from them as the other guy waded towards his colleague to pull him up to safety, which was all well and good, but the woman was now free and about to be sent sailing down the river at high speed, making her difficult to catch.

'Christ almighty,' muttered Ben, watching the display with a look of horror etched across his face. The other guy in the water was too busy helping his colleague to grab the loose rope, and no one else was dressed suitably to go into the freezing water, but Morgan couldn't watch her get washed away. She kicked off her boots, which she hadn't laced up properly, shrugged off her jacket and jumped in to the sound of Ben shouting at her.

'Morgan, you bloody idiot.'

She splashed towards the body, managing to snag hold of one arm. Gritting her teeth that were chattering loudly with the icy-cold, she fished in the water for the rope and then began wading towards the bank, soaking wet and shivering so much she thought that her teeth might fall out if she didn't let go. She tugged the body behind her until she was back at the side of the river. Two mountain rescue guys reached down to pull her out. She passed another the rope and then she was being pulled out of the river. She was shivering so much she thought she might shake her brains out, and then she was wrapped in a silver blanket and Ben had his arms around her.

'We need to get you back to Ettie's.'

She nodded, unable to speak. She was sodden and mind-numbingly cold, and she let him drag her through the trees, but not before she glanced back and double checked that they had a tight hold of the body and the woman was being pulled out of the water back to safety this time.

'What were you thinking? That was so dangerous.'

She looked down at her bare feet: which was worse, the pain from the fallen pine needles and branches sticking in the soles of her feet or the treacherous cold from the water? She wasn't sure, everything hurt, but she managed to make it back to the cottage where Ettie was standing at the front door with eyes open wide, shaking her head. She disappeared inside then was coming towards them with a huge blanket and some slippers for Morgan's feet. She got into the cottage and Ettie commanded, 'Strip out of those wet clothes now.'

Morgan did as she was told, glad she had no buttons to unfasten as her fingers were trembling that much. Ettie had a huge soft bath sheet that she held in front of her as Ben helped to remove her leggings. Within seconds she was wrapped in the soft, fluffy towel, another blanket around her and led to the chair closest to the wood-burning stove. When she was sitting in front of it, her teeth still chattered, but the warmth was making her feel better.

Ettie asked, 'What happened, did you fall in?'

Morgan's teeth were unable to let her talk properly, and Ben replied for her. 'They accidentally let go of the rope around the body and it was floating away, so Morgan jumped in after it and stopped it.'

Ettie smiled at her. 'Crazy, selfless and wonderful. Let me get you a brandy, it will warm you up in no time.'

Ben sat next to her, wrapping his arms around her, his body heat helping to warm her up. She accepted the glass of amber-coloured liquid from Ettie and took a huge gulp. Choking on it she began to cough and splutter, but the burning in the back of her throat did the trick and when she regained her composure, she realised she could form words again, her teeth were no longer clacking together.

'I'm not apologising.'

'I wouldn't expect you to, you saved the day. By the time they were ready to go back in the water, who knows where she could have ended up? Thank you, you were incredibly brave.'

'Not sure about brave, I think my nipples may have fallen off in that water it was so cold.'

Ben laughed, and Ettie smirked at her.

Morgan smiled at them. 'I couldn't watch her float away, she deserves better, Ben.'

'I know, she does.'

'It's lucky for her that she turned up here, because nobody will work harder than us to find out who she is and what happened to her.'

'That is very true.'

Ettie clapped her hands. 'Ah, you two are just so sweet. I'm so sad for her but I'm also happy that you were both here to help her. I know you will find her family and get her home.'

Morgan's thoughts went back to the dead woman; she didn't want to have to tell her family that they'd lost her, and yet she didn't want the girl to be all alone with no one to care about what had happened to her. She didn't think her heart could bear it if she was.

SIX

Declan saw Cain waiting for him at the car park and waved to him. As they made their way to the scene, they heard all about the dramatic rescue Morgan had made firsthand from one of the mountain rescue guys who was on his way back to their 4x4.

'That copper jumped into that freezing river without even thinking about it. It was totally epic; I've never seen anything like it. I mean the poor woman was a bit slippery and she's already lost the skin off one hand.'

Declan looked at Cain, who replied, 'Can't believe we missed that; Morgan is nuts, you wouldn't get me jumping in that river to drag a dead body out.'

Declan shook his head, he would probably have done the same, but he was concerned for Morgan. 'Where is she?'

'Her aunt's cottage probably. Lucky for her she lives around here, otherwise you might have two bodies to deal with.'

'Quite. I'll take a look at the body, then I'll go speak to Morgan.'

They walked straight into Ben who had a grim expression on his face, causing Declan a mild flutter of panic inside his chest. Ever since Theo's attack he seemed to have softened a little around the edges and found himself worrying about his friends a lot more than he used to. 'How's Morgan? One of the guys from mountain rescue just told us.'

'Cold, but okay.'

Cain shook his head. 'Best part of the day and I missed it. Did she strip off first?'

Ben glared at him, even Declan looked shocked.

'Oh, that's not what I meant. I mean did she at least take her boots off, because you know it's like they're welded to her feet and if she didn't, well, she's lucky she didn't drown too.'

'Shut up, Cain, you're not helping,' growled Ben.

Cain's cheeks burned red, and he stopped talking. He took a paper bag full of pick and mix out of his pocket and offered it to Ben, who peered inside at the assorted boiled sweets and took out a lemon sherbet. Declan chose a mint, Cain's peace offering appreciated. Cain popped a large aniseed twist into his mouth. Ben turned to Declan.

'I'm not sure there's a lot you can do here to be honest. It's obvious she was deceased, and I think she has been for some time, so you may have been called out for nothing. I think she might have been in the water too long for forensics.'

Declan shrugged. 'No matter, and we won't know for sure until I get her into my mortuary. I've managed to get DNA off previously submerged bodies, so it's always a possibility depending upon various environmental factors. Besides, I'm here, I may as well take a look but maybe you should tell the control room inspector to take my number off speed dial; it seems the minute someone dies they ring me and call me out even when I'm not needed.' He winked at Ben. 'Unless you requested me, and that's a different matter, I am always here for you, my friend.'

'Not me, mate, I was too busy trying to get here to make sure Morgan's aunt was okay. She's the one who found her.'

'Oh no, feck. Poor Ettie, she's been through a lot lately, this is all she needed.'

'She's tougher than she looks. I suppose it's a family trait.'

Declan smiled. 'Yes, you look at Morgan and see this adorable woman with her tattoos and Doc Martens, and you would never guess that she's a seasoned detective with a heart of gold and a head made of steel. The girl is a feisty one when she has to be.'

Ben laughed. 'Yes, just like Ettie.'

'I suppose that's a good thing then. Come on, lead me to my next patient.'

They walked in a line to the narrow clearing where the woman was now inside of a body bag. Ben began explaining, 'She was found caught up in that fallen tree. Ettie said she thinks it's only been there a few weeks, since the tree came down in the storm.'

'Are we thinking a drowning?'

Ben shrugged. 'No idea, I'll let you figure that one out. We haven't had any missing person reports, but Amy is doing all the checks back at the station.'

Declan walked as close to the edge as possible. Morgan's empty boots were sitting there and he smiled to see them, it looked as if they were standing guard. The riverbank was a mess of footprints, and he turned to Ben. 'Did you see it before everyone trampled all over it? Did she go into the water here do you think?'

'I did, but I didn't notice anything remotely suspicious or out of place. The thing is, Declan, one of her hands is skeletonised yet the rest of her looks pretty intact, and like I said, I think she's been dead for some time.'

Declan was crouching down to look at the body, and Cain leaned over him as he unzipped the bag and pulled it wide. Cain opened his mouth to speak and his sweet fell straight out of it and landed somewhere inside of the bag. He straightened up quickly and whispered, 'Oh my God.'

Ben narrowed his eyes. 'What?'

Both Ben and Declan were staring at Cain. 'What's the matter?' Ben asked. 'Do you know her?'

Cain shook his head. 'No, it's not that. I, erm, I dropped my sweet in there.' He was pointing into the body bag, staring in horror at Ben.

Declan began to laugh.

'It's not funny, the only DNA you're going to get is off me and I've never seen her before in my life.'

Ben cupped a hand over his own mouth, turning slightly so Cain couldn't see the grin on his face. Declan was still laughing but Cain looked mortified.

'I'm sure Angela will come visit you in prison,' Ben whispered as Wendy came stomping towards them.

'What's so funny and who documented the scene?'

Ben pointed to the fire officer who had a bodycam. 'He did and one of the mountain rescue guys as well. We couldn't wait for you to get here; we had to get her out of the water ASAP. I thought it was your day off too?'

'It was, but apparently Joe is at another job and there was nobody apart from Carlisle who wouldn't be here for another couple of hours. Control rang me and I offered to come in.'

Ben clamped an arm around her shoulders. 'You are a right softie underneath that angry exterior.'

She shook her head. 'Maybe, but I care about you all and—'

'You're too nosy for your own good,' said Cain.

She glared at him. 'Why were you all laughing?'

Declan pointed to Cain. 'Somewhere inside of that body bag is his extra-large boiled sweet that dropped out of his mouth.'

'Oh my God, that's like completely gross. Cain, you're disgusting.'

Declan was still smiling. 'If you pass me a pair of tweezers, I'll see if I can get it back for you, Cain.' He winked at him, and Cain mimed throwing up.

Wendy was staring at them all in turn. 'What is wrong with you people?' She shook her head and left them to go talk to the fire officer.

Declan studied the woman, looking sadly and seriously at the body. The skeletal hand. The pale skin. 'I need to get her on the table. Since she's been moved, there's nothing I can really tell you out here, but I am fascinated by the lack of flesh on her right hand. You know me, I like a challenge, and I think this may be a tricky one. If you find a point of entry or somewhere she may have been lying before she got washed into the river, a forensic botanist might be able to help with soil samples, but depending on how long she's been in the water your initial observations about a lack of forensics may be correct, Ben, but let's see what we can do.'

'I thought as much, I'm sorry you were called out for no reason.'

'Ha, it was worth it though for that little jewel of a mishap that Cain happened to perform. I have never had a more serious case of inappropriate giggles in a long time. I never said there was no reason, I'm just erring on the side of caution and not wanting to get your hopes up too much, Ben. I'll speak to you later. Susie is on hand to book her in. I'm going home to see Theo.'

'How is he?'

Declan shrugged. 'Better and worse than I thought. He seems to be struggling with it all.' He lowered his voice. 'How does Morgan do it? How does she cope with everything that's happened to her and still turn up for work?'

'I think they broke the mould when they made her, I have no idea. Maybe you could invite her out for a coffee and chat about it. She never discusses it with me, but I bet she would with you. It might help you understand more of what Theo is going through and that can only be a good thing.'

'Yes, I might do that. Thanks.' He lifted a hand and waved before turning and heading back to his car, leaving Ben wondering: how did Morgan cope with all the stuff that had happened to her?

SEVEN

Declan found Ettie's cottage and smiled. It reminded him of something the bad witch in a fairy tale would live in, only he knew Ettie was a good person – a self-pronounced witch she may be but wicked she was not. He watched the huge black raven sitting on the fence with eyes wide, it was staring right back at him. It didn't even take off when he opened the gate, its small, black eyes following his every movement. He held up his hands. 'I'm a friend, what are you, some kind of attack bird?'

'Only if he has to be.'

Morgan's voice made Declan's pulse race a little faster. He hadn't been expecting her to be there and for a split second he'd thought it was the bird who'd spoken. He laughed, a little nervously, hearing the slight quiver in his voice.

'You scared the bejesus out of me, Morgan. What are you doing creeping up on me like that? I'm an older guy, you could have killed me off.'

'Declan, you're only a few years older than me.'

He put one hand on his hip. 'Am I now, I'm in my forties like your lover boy. I'm a man of the world.'

She rolled her eyes at him and opened the door so he could

come in out of the cold. Declan bent down, brushing his lips against the soft skin of Morgan's cheek. Her aunt was standing there, and he couldn't help himself, he walked straight over to her and hugged her.

'Ettie, how are you after that terrible shock?'

'I feel terrible for that poor woman, but I'm okay in myself.'

'Good, I'm glad. I can see where our Morgan gets her toughness from. She takes after you in brains and beauty.'

Ettie laughed, and he thought he saw Morgan's lip upturn a little. She was wanting to smile but giving him a hard time. He liked that, he loved her feisty attitude; he loved her but not in a romantic way because he wasn't into women. He loved her like he imagined it would be to have an annoying little sister who you secretly worshipped but would never admit that to them.

'I have nothing I can tell you except that her body has been recovered out of the water and will soon be on her way to my spot, where Susie is waiting to take very good care of her.'

Ettie nodded. 'That's good, I'm glad she's out of that freezing river.'

'Me too, not a nice place to be.'

'Would you like a cup of tea or coffee, Declan?'

He wondered if he should, did he have another ten minutes to spare to sit with these two glorious women? He wanted to, but something told him to get back to Theo. He was so worried about him. 'I'd love to, but Theo is waiting for me, so I'll have to say no this time, but next time I'm passing I'll take you up on that offer.'

'You pass here often?'

'Morgan, don't be so picky. I like to wander in the woods. I might bring Theo for some fresh air on my next weekend off.'

Ettie took hold of his hand. 'Well then, if you do make sure you and Theo call here for a hot drink and some cake. I would love to see you both.'

'Cake? We'll be here, if you ask me there isn't enough cake

eaten in this world, it's such a glorious food. It never fails to cheer a person up when there's cake being passed around.'

Ettie excused herself and left him standing looking at Morgan with desperation in his eyes.

She lowered her voice. 'Is everything okay?'

He shrugged. 'I'm worried about Theo; he's acting really odd. He doesn't want to leave the house, is spending all day in the bedroom staring out of the window, and I don't know what to do about it.'

'Would you like me to come and see him tomorrow, if I can? If not tomorrow, as soon as I get a minute.'

'Yes, please. He's not talking about his attack to me, but he might open up to you. He knows how much you've been through.'

The flush of a toilet upstairs and footsteps as Ettie came back down made Declan step towards the door. About to leave, he turned back to Ettie. 'Did you notice if she was wearing a coat?'

Ettie shook her head. 'I think I was so shocked I didn't take a proper look.'

'That's okay, I can't believe she just fell into the water. In this weather she would be dressed much warmer, if she was out walking, wouldn't she?'

'Unless the coat came off with the churning water and is stuck in a fallen branch further downstream,' replied Morgan.

'Maybe, I'll let you and Ben work that one out.'

He gave her another quick squeeze, then walked out of the door to see the bird was still sitting on the fence watching him. That bird was definitely better at guarding than most dogs.

EIGHT

He had known buying the two industrial freezers was at some point going to be a worthwhile investment, though he hadn't known that it wasn't animal meat he would be storing in them, but it was swings and roundabouts. He regretted the combination locks he'd fitted to them; they were a pain in the arse. His fingers were a little too chubby to be able to whiz them around deftly. It always took a couple of attempts before he lined the numbers up perfectly. He hadn't realised he was muttering to himself until the final o slipped into place and it sprang open.

He had to lock them, as his mother was a nightmare and too inquisitive for her own good. He smiled to himself, though it would be fun to see the expression on her face as she lifted the lid, just like he was doing now. He smiled down at the face staring up at him, her expression one of mild shock, the tiny ice crystals on her eyelashes and thick black eyebrows making her look like something out of a fairy tale, The Snow Queen perhaps. She had been pretty once, before the drugs and alcohol had taken its toll on her skin, but now, she was frozen in time and space and she looked more like her old self. The blue tinge to her lips gave her an almost ethereal look, his little snow angel.

He leaned down, sucking his stomach in so he could reach her frozen face, and kissed her forehead, his lips brushing the ice.

'What are you doing in there? Did you get the mince out for tomorrow?'

He grimaced, curled his fist and pretended to smash his mother's face in with it as he punched the air. Slamming the freezer door shut, he snapped the lock back into place and went to the chest freezer that they did use for keeping the shopping in – all those yellow stickered out-of-date bargains she would spend hours hunting down in every supermarket in the area. He imagined that one day he would shove her into a freezer too, but not one with his angels inside. She would corrupt them with her vicious thoughts and vile mouth. She would be on her own, where she should be, and if she wouldn't be missed at church he would have done it a long time ago.

Staring longingly at the second freezer, he regretted that he didn't have time to look inside of this one, but tomorrow when the old bitch was out, he would come down here and spend some time with his ice girls. He had an old armchair that he would sit in and talk to them; they never answered but that was how he liked it. The only woman he had in his life couldn't shut up to save her soul. He wondered how they coped with her at their new church and her rabbiting on and on about all the inconsequential crap that filled her brain. Giving one last glance at his girls he smiled, those freezers had been the best bargain he'd ever got. The butchers on the high street had shut down and sold everything off. He was lucky he'd walked past that particular day, because they served their purpose well and as long as he didn't choose women who were too tall there was no problem keeping their bodies inside of them.

He locked the door to the garage behind him, tucking the key into his pocket. They didn't have a car that would fit inside of it – whoever built it didn't think a car bigger than a Mini Cooper was a necessity. His estate was far too long to drive into it. He didn't want to risk leaving the freezers accessible, although he did have to back up into it in the dark a week ago to drag the body out of the freezer and drive it to the river.

He hadn't wanted to part with her if he was honest because she had been his first, but he needed the space. The river was the only place he could think where she would defrost nicely, and if there was any of that DNA on her, that would wash off too.

He wasn't some master criminal, he didn't watch the cop shows or anything like that, but he knew enough through reading the newspapers that it was that DNA stuff that connected killers to victims, and he wasn't crazy enough to do anything like that.

NINE

As Morgan left Ettie's cottage, she saw Ben heading down the path towards her. 'What's happening?'

'Body has gone to the mortuary; we've got the woods sealed off and Task Force are going to do a full area search, but it's a lot of ground to cover. Al said he can send a drone up but with all the trees it's not going to see much, dog handler is on the way to help. Mountain rescue have offered to help with the search to see if they can find a point of entry into the water, footprints, drag marks, tyre marks, clothing that has been discarded, which is very good of them.'

'Have you said yes?'

Ben nodded. 'Be foolish to turn them down, the quicker we cover this area to see if there are any forensics the better.'

'Do you think there will be any? Forensics?'

He shrugged. 'I wouldn't like to place a bet on there being any, no. I'm thinking maybe she could have fallen in.'

'Wouldn't someone be missing her if she had?'

'Not everyone has someone that misses them. Some people are all alone in this world with no family or friends.'

'Yes, they are but still. There's something very wrong about this, Ben, I can feel it. For what it's worth I think she was pushed in or dumped there and killed before she even hit the water. Someone, somewhere knows something.'

He nodded, trying not to smile at her despite the sadness of the situation. 'That's a lot of, what do you call it, alliteration?'

'I read a lot, I'm highly intelligent.' She winked at him. 'So, what are we doing?'

'I literally have no idea.' He was staring past her at Ettie's garden gate, and she knew he was thinking about cake or biscuits, maybe both because Ettie always had a supply of both.

'I think we need to go back to the station and talk this through, see if Amy has found anything, let the professionals get on with the search. It's not as if there are any house-to-house enquiries around here and we have a full statement off Ettie.'

Morgan couldn't see the river from where she was standing, but could hear the urgent rush of the water as it crashed against the rocks and flowed downstream not too far away. She knew the area was remote, but she wanted to double check what other homes were in the vicinity.

'There's one house that has this part of the river running through the bottom of their garden.'

A sharp pain lodged in her chest at the thought of the Potter family, Bronte's violent, tragic death still fresh in her mind, an open wound she didn't think would ever heal. Ben let out a long sigh.

'Of course, the Potters' old house, although I don't think they could possibly have seen anything, but we better go speak to them just in case they have a camera or something facing the woods.'

A part of Morgan wished she hadn't reminded him. To return to that house, where she found almost the entire family murdered, except for Bronte – who had been clinging on to life – was something that she had never forgot. Her first day out on independent patrol and she had gone willingly to the shout for a possible suicide that had turned into familicide. The house had finally been sold; she had no idea who had bought it after it had lain empty for over twelve months, but someone hadn't cared enough about its history to let that deter them.

'I can go on my own if you'd rather not. You can wait in the car, it's no bother.'

She shook her head, brave, foolish, feisty, reckless were all words that could be used to describe Morgan, but coward wasn't one and she would never let herself be called that under any circumstances. 'I'm good, I'll come with you.'

The gates at the entrance to the Potters' drive were wide open so Ben drove straight through. Morgan purposely avoided looking at the old tree where Olivia Potter had been found hanging, instead staring at the house which looked a little unloved. It had been freshly renovated, the outside a gleaming white that fateful day she arrived at the scene. Now, the paint was dull, a dirty grey, and the windows that had sparkled looked as if they hadn't been cleaned in a long time. There was a van parked outside for a building supply company, and she recognised the bright blue and yellow logo, knowing they had recently opened a branch in Kendal. The front door was wide open, and Morgan's heart was pounding so loud in her chest she could feel her ribcage vibrating.

Before she could change her mind, she got out of Ben's BMW. Before Ben was even out of the car she was knocking loudly on the open door.

'Hello, it's the police, is anyone there?'

A guy appeared from the kitchen doorway, a half-eaten sandwich in one hand and a mug of coffee in the other. A look of confusion etched across his face as he stared at her.

'Can I help you?' He sounded unsure of himself, looking

like he had no idea what she was doing here or why the police would be hammering on the door.

'Do you live here?' Morgan expected him to say no, then realised a delivery driver wouldn't be making his lunch in a customer's house. He nodded.

'I do, why?'

'I'm Detective Constable Morgan Brookes and this is my colleague, DS Ben Matthews, we're investigating a drowning in the river that runs through your land and wondered if you had any cameras on the property that might look in that direction.'

She smiled at him, not a full smile, but just enough to make her seem friendly and not as scary as she was acting. He was staring at her, but when Ben appeared behind her, the guy gave him his attention.

'You found a body in the river? That's awful, poor bugger. How did they get there?'

Ben arched an eyebrow at Morgan, who ignored him.

'That's what we're trying to determine.'

'Oh, that's terribly sad. No, I don't have cameras, well not any that work anyway. There are a couple that were already up, but I don't have access to them or the passcodes. The family here before me installed them, and I haven't taken them down because they look the part even if they're useless.'

For a moment she wondered if he knew about the tragic history of this house.

'The Potters?'

He nodded. 'Yeah, terrible what happened to them. Why don't you come in, can I get you guys a hot drink or something?'

Despite how cold it was outside and how Morgan's finger-tips were almost numb, she would rather not go back into the house. Ben stepped past her.

'That would be great, thank you.'

He walked in, following the guy, leaving Morgan no room to say no. She stepped into the hall and tried to stop the images of what she had found downstairs in the cellar from causing her brain to overload. Instead, she looked around, noticing the recent changes. The walls were painted a rich green colour, she liked it. The smell of fresh paint lingered in the air.

Ben was already in the kitchen sitting on a chair as she entered it. The aroma of freshly brewed coffee smelled amazing; it never failed to spark something inside of her and make her brain function better. Ben had taken over the conversation and she let him, still trying to process how she felt about being back inside this *house of horror* as the local paper had daubed it in big, bold typeface on the front page.

'I bought it some time ago; I wasn't sure what I was going to do with it. I did think about renting it out, maybe on Airbnb, but then I split up with my wife and thought I'd live here whilst I got my act together.'

He passed them both a mug of coffee, then took a carton of milk out of the fridge and put it on the table. The words were out of Morgan's mouth before she could stop them.

'You know about the history of this house, and it doesn't bother you?'

Ben side-eyed her, and she shrugged.

The guy nodded. 'I do, it's tragic and very sad, but it's not the house's fault. I get why a lot of people passed on buying it, but it was a very good price and I'm not into ghosts or stuff like that, for one thing I haven't got the time to worry about being haunted. I work all day, come home and start painting or stripping walls, so by the time I fall into bed no ghost is going to wake me up.'

Morgan looked at him and thought, *famous last words.*

'What?' The guy who had been finishing his sandwich asked her through a mouthful of food, and she realised she'd said that out loud.

'Nothing, sorry. Talking to myself.'

Ben looked horrified and turned away from her.

'What's your name for our records, mate?'

'Jonah Silver, but everyone calls me Jon.'

Ben was writing in his notebook. 'Thanks, is that Jon with an h or without? Where did you live before you moved here?'

'Without. I lived in Ulverston, loved it but I wanted to get as far away from Janine, my ex, as I could. It's a small town and everyone knows your business; it's a shame I didn't realise what was going on before everyone else did.

'I'm really sorry, but I work six days a week then when I'm here I'm painting. I'm not superstitious or anything but I wanted to put my own stamp on the house, change the colour scheme, carpets, that kind of thing. Gives me something to do when I'm stuck here on my own wondering what my ex is getting up to. I have no idea what's happened down at the river and I'm kind of glad that I don't. I haven't even walked down there since the day I got the keys, the weather has been too shite, all this rain and now the snow and frost that we keep getting. The riverbank is muddy and treacherous, and knowing my luck I'd fall in, which is probably what happened to whoever you found.'

'It is a possibility and yes, that's not so good, is it? Thank you for the coffee.' Ben tipped the mug and drained the last drops; Morgan had only taken a few sips. He stood up. 'We best get on, good luck with the painting.'

Morgan smiled at him, took another sip and stood. 'I like the green in the hallway.'

'Thanks, apparently it's all the fashion according to the Instagram accounts I follow.'

This really made her smile, and she nodded. Black was her colour of choice, closely followed by muted greens and a little pale pink. Cain's partner, Angela, had the pinkest house she had ever seen, and she loved it, something she never thought she would.

They left Jon to head back to the station, Morgan feeling a

little better after being inside the house and surviving the memories all over again. They say that every cop has a case that haunts them and for her it would always be this one, and she hoped that the Potters weren't stuck here in some kind of limbo. Now they had all been reunited, she hoped they'd been able to move on to a much better place.

TEN

Declan walked into the vicarage and the smell of freshly baked cake hit his nostrils, making his stomach groan in appreciation. Had Theo been baking? The thought made his heart a little warmer than it was when he'd left. The kitchen light was on, and he walked into it not sure if he would find the love of his life or one of the women from the lady's group that had managed to get in through the front door. Theo turned to him and smiled; Declan smiled back.

'Hello, I have to say I'm relieved not to find one of the ladies from the Father Theo appreciation fan club in here making cakes. What are you doing?'

His eyes fell onto the tray of muffins that were cooling on the side.

'I have a visitor calling tomorrow who I haven't seen in a long time, and I thought I'd bake, as we had nothing decent in to offer them with a cup of tea.'

'That's great, but where did you get the stuff from? Has it always been lurking in the cupboard, and if it has why have you not baked since we first met?'

Theo grinned at him. 'I had a walk to the Co-op; I felt so

much better getting some fresh air although it's pretty nippy outside, but I wore a hat to cover the mess at the back of my head, so I didn't upset anyone.'

Declan strode across the large kitchen and pulled him in for a hug. 'I am so proud of you and those smell amazing. Can I eat one? For some strange reason I have been thinking about cake a lot today and then boom, I come home to freshly baked cakes, it's truly a miracle.'

Theo hugged him back, then let go and took one of the muffins out of the tray.

'Careful, they're a bit warm.'

Declan inhaled, closing his eyes in pleasure. Then tore the baking case from it and stuffed half of it in his mouth. 'Oh my God,' he said through a mouthful of cake, then shrugged an apology to Theo about using God's name that way, which made Theo laugh.

'They are that good?'

Shoving the rest of it in his mouth he nodded.

'God would highly approve.' They were that good, but even if they'd tasted awful, he would have acted the same way to make Theo feel better about something and see that cheeky grin; he would have pretended sawdust was tasty. When he could speak without spraying mashed-up cake crumbs everywhere, he did. 'They are divine, I'd forgot how good you are at baking, it's been that long. I knew I'd chosen the right guy the first time you whipped out your oven gloves and took that tray of shortbread out of the oven.'

Theo's loud laugh filled Declan's heart with hope that this was his turning point, that he might just be getting the old Theo back and for that he would have given anything. The morose, quiet, moody Theo had been hard to figure out and it hurt Declan deeply that none of this had been Theo's fault – he had been an innocent victim and almost paid with his life.

'So, who is this visitor? Is it some VIP or someone famous?'

Theo shook his head. 'No, just an old friend, well he was more of a volunteer at the church. He used to come help out with his mum five days a week and was, is, a great guy. I think you'll like him.'

Declan felt a tiny stabbing pain inside his chest. Was he jealous of some old friend of Theo's? He didn't really do jealousy but wasn't sure what was going on.

'I have to ask, forgive my prying, is he an old lover?'

Theo shook his head. 'No, absolutely not. He is definitely a heterosexual kind of guy, but would it matter if he was? Why are you asking that? What has it got to do with anything?'

'No, it wouldn't. I'm happy to see you pottering around, baking of all things, so if the thought of him calling has given you a reason to get out of these four walls for a little bit and bake scrumptious cakes, I can't wait to meet him.'

'Scrumptious, did you actually say that out loud? You sound more like a vicar than I do.'

Declan felt his cheeks begin to burn but laughed all the same. 'That did sound a bit vicarish. You're having a bad, or is it a good, effect on me?'

He took hold of Theo's hand. 'Seriously, I'm so happy to see you happy.'

'Will you be here tomorrow when he calls?'

'Probably not, unless you need me to be here. I have a full day tomorrow and now that a body has been found in the river, I'm going to need to sort that out too.'

Theo shook his head. 'No, I don't need you, I just wondered, and how was it, bad?'

Declan thought that Theo looked kind of relieved at that, and something niggled away at his chest again. He had to push the feeling away, tamp it down.

'It was sad, more than anything. What an awful way to die if she did that way, slipping into a river and being unable to save yourself is horrid. So, what's for tea or can we just eat all the cakes and make ourselves sick with all the sugar?'

'What do you fancy?'

Declan looked into Theo's eyes. 'You.'

Theo didn't turn away; he looked right back. 'Good, that's nice to know. But I won't fit in the oven.' He winked at Declan who took a moment to realise he was cracking more jokes, and he liked it.

He sounded more like his old self and that could only be a good thing.

'I would take far too long to cook, and I'm hungry. Should we order pizza or Thai?'

'Pizza.'

'Pizza it is.' Declan took out his phone to order the pizza as Theo opened the oven door and took out a tray of flapjacks. Tucking his phone under his ear, he put his hands together, bending his fingers in the shape of a heart.

Theo mouthed, 'I love you too,' back at him.

ELEVEN

The DI was sitting in the CID office when Morgan and Ben walked in. Morgan knew it was his day off by his lack of a suit and tie; he was wearing a Nike hoodie, joggers and trainers, which actually made him look relaxed for once – that, and the fact that he was slumped on a chair scrolling through his phone and not pacing up and down like he usually did.

'What are you doing here, Marc?'

He smiled at her. 'I could ask you the same. I thought you put a half day in to go to the spa with Wendy. I should have known you wouldn't be able to relax.'

She shrugged. 'My aunt rang me; I had to go.'

He nodded slowly. 'My boss rang me; I had to come in too. Bummer or what?'

Morgan wanted to laugh; he was getting good at cracking jokes, but she didn't want to make his head swell because he already loved himself enough. Unable to stop herself she felt the sides of her mouth curl up, and he pointed at her.

'I don't know why you try not to find my jokes funny, Morgan, especially when you know they are, but I'm going to keep working on you until you actually manage to let out a full-blown laugh.'

Cain walked in carrying a tray with mugs and a half-eaten packet of biscuits. 'You're not that funny, boss, everyone knows I'm the funny guy so don't get too cocky about it.'

Marc rolled his eyes at Amy who was shaking her head at them all.

She muttered, 'It's like working in a school with you lot. I don't get paid enough for this.'

Cain placed a mug on her desk. 'You don't get paid enough, you get paid too much if you ask me, sitting there with a face like a slapped arse all day and not even bothering to brew up. It's your own fault you got yourself up the duff, not ours.'

Morgan, Ben and Marc all turned to see if Amy was going to get up and punch Cain for being so cheeky. Instead, she gave him the v's and grinned.

'You have a way with words, Cain. I can't wait for your next sentence, and where did you steal those biscuits from?'

'Didn't steal them, Brenda donated them to me. She said to keep you well fed because you're like a gremlin.'

Morgan stepped in between them to defuse the situation before Amy decided she'd definitely had enough and decked Cain for good measure. Marc took one of the mugs from the tray.

'So, what's the general consensus, accidental or suspicious death?' He looked around at their faces.

'Suspicious,' said Morgan with no hesitation.

'Not sure,' replied Ben.

'Twenty quid says accidental,' said Cain.

Amy, who hadn't even stopped shaking her head at him from his last sentence, said, 'You are disgusting, Cain, some poor woman has been found in the river in these freezing temperatures, who nobody has bothered to report missing, and you're taking bets on how she died.'

Marc pulled out his wallet, took a twenty pound note out, and passed it to Cain. 'Accidental.'

Morgan glared at the two men. 'You two are sick.'

Cain shrugged. 'Come on, Morgan, it's just a bit of fun in this never-ending world of bleakness that we have to endure on a daily basis.'

Ben looked surprised. 'Wow, you almost sound intelligent, Cain. Has Angela been making you read actual books?'

Cain tutted loudly. 'For your information, I read quite a lot on my days off. I just don't talk about it all the time and bore everyone to death like some people I could mention.'

Morgan turned to him. 'What are you reading now?'

'*Message Deleted* by K.L. Slater.'

'Oh, wow. I'm impressed, that's next on my to-be-read list.'

His smile was smug. 'I'm not a total idiot, and Angela made me read it, said it was excellent.'

Marc rolled his eyes. 'Yes, well now that we have proof you have a fully functional brain inside that extra thick skull, what are we doing about the body in the river?'

Ben shrugged. 'Waiting on the post-mortem results tomorrow. I tell you what does concern me though. How does she have one hand that is skeletal? Three of those fingers had no flesh on them yet the rest of her is intact.'

'Animals? Maybe something had a nibble at her,' Marc said between sips of his coffee.

Ben shook his head. 'What, and they left the rest of her? Unless she got caught nearer to the riverbank and something did, but I don't know if I buy that, and as far as I know there are no piranha fish in the river.'

'Interesting, maybe I should have gone with suspicious.' Marc was smiling at Morgan, and she turned away from him to face Amy.

'Did you find any logs for mispers out of county?'

Amy nodded. 'Lots of them, but none of them match the

description we have from the first officer on the scene: blonde hair, mid-forties, slim build, Caucasian. There are a couple from years ago in the right age range, which I've printed out and put on your desk, Ben. I don't think they will match the body though.'

'Maybe not, but I'll take a look. Thanks, Amy. Boss, I don't think there's much need for you to be honest. We'll know more tomorrow after the PM, you might as well salvage what you can of your rest day.'

Marc drained his mug and stood up. 'See you tomorrow then, but if you need me, ring me.'

He left them, and Cain whispered, 'Do you buy that? Why would they call him in for this? It's not a confirmed murder and there's a DI covering from Barrow who was on the phone earlier when I got to the scene.'

Amy walked to the door and, pushing it open, stared out into the empty corridor then let the door shut behind her before speaking. 'I think he's trying a little too hard to fit in. Seems a bit desperate if you ask me.'

Morgan shook her head. 'Maybe he is, but at least he's dropped the I'm a big city cop who knows more than you do, and trying. Maybe he asked Control to ring him if anything cropped up.'

Ben held up his hands to stop them. 'And maybe you lot need to stop gossiping and start working. Let's get this Jane Doe identified and her family notified as soon as we can, so whoever is missing her can finally get some closure. I'm going to see if Wendy can go to the mortuary and get her fingerprints or a DNA sample so we can check our databases.'

Morgan didn't mention that Wendy might have a difficult time with only one set of fingers still intact with the flesh on them, but Ben didn't seem to be in such a great mood.

TWELVE

The office door opened, and Scotty stood there staring at Cain, Amy and Morgan. Amber was standing behind him and she gave him a gentle push and then followed him in, letting the door close. 'Tell them what you just told me?'

He frowned at her. 'I'm going to, Christ, you're worse than my wife.'

'Your wife is a saint. I literally have no idea how she puts up with you.'

He ignored Amber and his eyes rested on Morgan, who he must have deemed was going to be the kindest out of them all to him. 'I was there a couple of weeks ago.'

Cain, Amy and Morgan all stared at him, and she asked. 'Where?'

'The car park to Covel Woods. I was taking my son for a walk and there was this couple who were arguing next to their car. It wasn't violent but it was loud, a bit too loud for a quiet woodland walk if you know what I mean, but I had Sam with me and it was my day off, so there was no way I was getting involved in a non-violent domestic when my son was with me; he's only six and it wouldn't have been fair on him.'

Amber snorted. 'There's no way you'd get involved in a non-violent domestic when it wasn't your day off, what are you talking about?'

The scowl on his face told Morgan that he had clearly had enough of Amber. 'Why don't you come and talk to me about it in Ben's office, he's not there.'

'We know, we passed him in the corridor, which is why he's here now. He's scared of Ben.'

'Shut up, Amber,' Scotty growled.

Morgan grabbed his elbow and guided him towards the office. Amber turned around, lowering her voice, 'If it turns out it's the woman he ignored and she got murdered, that's going to be awkward. He'll get suspended, you know what this place is like. He'll have PSD breathing down his neck before he's even walked out of the car park.'

Then she was out of there, and Morgan closed Ben's door behind them.

'You know people argue all the time, so the chance that it's the same woman is very slim. Did you get a description of her? Would you know her if you saw her again?'

Morgan was wondering if they should get him to go to the mortuary to look at the body in case it was.

He shrugged. 'I couldn't say for sure; I didn't stare at them. You know what it's like when you're arguing with your partner, you don't want some stranger gawping and interfering. She was blonde, mid-forties maybe, not very tall, it's hard to say. He was much taller than his partner, around Cain's size, dark brown hair; they had a rust-coloured car, a Vauxhall I think.'

'What made you look at them in the first place, you know, take notice?'

'She kept glancing over at me as if she was embarrassed. It was obvious they were arguing but I just pushed Sam along to the path and left them to it. I feel like crap now. What if he killed her and dumped her body in the river?'

'Do you think she was looking at you for help? Did she want you to intervene?'

He shook his head. 'No, it was more embarrassment. If she needed help, she only had to ask, and I would have stepped in then, but she didn't. She just kept giving me this side-eye as if she wanted me to get out of there with Sam.'

'Was the car still there when you came back from your walk?'

He shook his head. 'I don't think it was, but I didn't look to be honest. I kind of forgot about them. Sam is a bit of a handful so keeping him interested in a walk through the woods was a bit of a challenge. Then that shout came in before and I was on enquiries at the time, so I didn't offer to go, but then when I heard where it was, I got a bit worried and remembered the couple arguing, so here I am.'

'Thanks for coming forward with this, Scotty, Ben will probably want me to take a statement, but we can do it down-stairs in an empty room out of sight, so no one has to know, if you'd rather do that than sitting in here with everyone listening.'

He nodded; he looked miserable. 'Can we do it now and get it over with.'

'Of course, I'll be down in five minutes. Meet you down there, okay?'

When he'd left, she grabbed her laptop and charger.

Cain eyed her up. 'Should he have intervened?'

She shrugged. 'Who knows, probably not but we can't rule anything out. We won't know anything until tomorrow when Declan does her post-mortem. We need to find out who she is though because someone must be missing her.'

Before going down to Scotty she wondered if there were any other houses hidden away in the area that she wasn't aware of, who might have CCTV that covered the area; it was worth checking out. Logging on to her computer she brought up Google Maps of the area and found there were several houses along a stretch of road called Red Bank, but it was the opposite side of the woods to the entrance to the car park. Still, it might be worth getting the PCSOs to check out the properties to see if they had cameras that captured the woman walking past or the rust coloured Vauxhall leaving the area. Sending the map to print, she decided she would ask Madds or whoever was on duty to allocate it to the PCSOs on duty. Next, she opened Instagram and searched for the hashtag #covelwoods to see if there were any recent posts for the area. Nothing came up, which surprised her a little, though it had been worth checking.

Morgan stood up and made her way downstairs to go and take Scotty's statement, hoping that he hadn't witnessed the woman's final moments alive and not intervened, because the thought of that was just horrific.

THIRTEEN

Ben was in his office and Cain was the only one sitting at a desk when Morgan walked back in clutching Scotty's statement in one hand. 'Did you tell him what Scotty said?'

Cain shook his head. 'Didn't want to spoil your fun.'

'Where's Amy?'

'Midwife appointment.'

'Are you two still living together?'

He nodded. 'Yeah, she's actually okay out of work. Great cook, does the washing, cleans the bathroom. All the stuff I hate.'

'Cain, aren't you supposed to be doing that and letting her put her feet up?'

'No, she needs to burn off that angry energy she carries around all day some way. Besides I don't take any money off her. She's saving up for a deposit for a flat and she said it makes her feel better about it. I hate cooking and cleaning, so it's win-win.'

Morgan wondered at the pair of them cohabiting, they sniped and argued at each other most of the time in work.

'You really are a big softie, aren't you?'

'I like to think that it's because I'm a half-decent bloke. I have my faults, we all do, but you know, kindness is always a good thing and right now with that arsehole Jack ignoring her, she needs a bit of support. Don't ever tell her I said that though. She thinks she's some tough bird who can cope on her own, and I have every faith that she will, but a bit of company, someone on your side, is nice now and again. If I move in with Angela, which is probably going to be soon, I was going to let her stay in the house as long as she pays the mortgage. It's not too bad, cheaper than the rent on a flat and much bigger. I paid most of the mortgage off with the money my nan left me when she died, bless her, so Amy will be able to afford it, even on our wages.'

Morgan had to turn away and blink the tears that had formed in the corners of her eyes. She was getting too soft, too emotional lately.

As if Cain sensed that, he asked, 'What did Scotty have to say for himself? Now, he's unreal. I don't think he'd have stepped in if the guy had his hands around the woman's throat in front of him, he'll do anything to avoid paperwork.'

'He said he feels bad, but he had his kid with him. Would you intervene if you had a kid with you?'

'I would have at least asked her if she was okay.'

And Morgan knew that Cain would have, because he was that kind of guy. Ben was beckoning her, and she stepped into his office.

'Scotty came up before.'

'I know, I saw him and Amber. What did they want?'

'He witnessed a couple having an argument in the car park to the woods a few weeks ago when he was taking his son on a walk.'

Ben sat up. 'He did, what level of argument?'

'Angry words, no violence, he didn't intervene because he said he wasn't that concerned about it and didn't want to with his son being there.'

Ben rolled his eyes. Scotty's reputation was legendary: if he could pass on a job he would, he was so laid-back and had no motivation to do anything other than turn up for work, drink tea and drive around in the van all day. She could tell Ben was trying his best not to sigh out loud.

'Did he at least get a make and model of the car, registration, descriptions of the couple? Did you show him the pictures on my desk that Amy printed out of the current mispers on the system from out of force areas?'

'I didn't think there was much point, as she said they're cold cases and not from around here. It was a rust-coloured Vauxhall, possibly a Grandland but could have been the smaller version, a Mokka. No VRM; she was blonde, possibly in her forties, guy was as tall as Cain, brown hair and that's it.'

Ben did let out a loud sigh this time. 'What the hell, is that it? I suppose the missing women are from how many years ago?' He looked down at the pictures on his desk. 'These are from Birmingham and the Midlands area. Still, can you go find him and ask, just to be sure?'

She nodded and placed the statement form on the table that she'd printed out. 'Look, he said he feels terrible, but he really didn't think there was any cause for concern, and I feel a bit bad for him. People argue all the time, we bicker sometimes, it's not his fault if he didn't think there was anything untoward going on. Most of us would have done the same, especially on our day off.'

That wasn't technically true, she knew; they had attended a double murder a few doors down from their house not that long ago on their day off. Some coppers were never really off duty, and she guessed she and Ben fell into that category by default. She left him to go and find Scotty, this time with the pictures in her hand.

FOURTEEN

As they ate breakfast the next morning, Declan phoned Ben to tell him he was going to get started on the post-mortem straight away, and it was up to Ben if he wanted to attend, but he was erring on the side of it being a suspicious death. Ben told him he'd be there, and Morgan, who was buttering the bagel she had managed to salvage from the toaster before it had burned to a crisp, wished for once Ben had said no. She turned around and offered him half of it, but he screwed up his face.

'No, thanks, you can keep it. Look, I think it's pointless us both going to the post-mortem, and I felt bad so said I would. Do you want to keep on plugging away here, get a list from the PNC bureau of all the possible cars registered locally that could have been in the car park? We need to find this couple that were arguing and get them spoken to and ticked off the list. If you could find them that would be really helpful, then take Cain with you to go and speak to them. Is that okay with you?'

She tried to suppress the grin threatening to take over her whole face. 'Absolutely, I can do that. It might be like looking for a needle in a haystack though, but I'll give it my best shot. I mean, they could have been visitors from out of the area. I'll go through all the ANPR camera footage nearest to Covel Wood and see if I can get a match.'

'That's great, keep you out of mischief too.'

'Who said I can't get into any, it's my speciality.'

'I know, that's why I said it.'

'Is it okay to pop in and see Theo at some point? Declan mentioned he's struggling and that a visit from me might be helpful.'

'Of course, give him my love and maybe on our next days off they could come here for something to eat, get him out of the house for a bit.'

She nodded. 'As long as you don't expect me to cook, Ben.'

He stared at the cremated bagel and smiled at her. 'I definitely don't expect you to cook, Morgan, I don't want to add food poisoning to his list of problems. He has enough without forcing your cooking onto him.'

She picked up the tea towel that was hooked over the rail on the cooker door and threw it in his direction. Ben ducked, jumped off the chair and chased her out of the kitchen. When he caught hold of her, he pulled her close and kissed her fiercely. Morgan kissed him back, unable to break away. When he finally did, he sighed.

'If only we had the time to go back to bed, I could show you some tricks with that tea towel.'

'Could you now, not sure what you're going to do with that tiny piece of cloth, but I'd love to see.'

'Clearly, I would use it to tie your wrists together and then I'd kiss you slowly from your toes all the way up to your lips.'

'Hm, I might just hold you to that next time we get a day off together.'

He let her go but was still grinning at her. 'Good, I should hope so. It's a promise.'

'I never knew you were into a bit of bondage, the more I get to know you the more you surprise me.'

'I am not into bondage; I just like the thought of having you in one place where you can't move for a little while. Oh, that sounds like I'm some kind of weirdo, forget I said that.'

Morgan laughed. 'Yeah, but you're *my* weirdo. I'm going to get dressed, I'll let you know if we find the couple who Scotty saw arguing in the car park. Say hi to Declan for me.'

Ben nodded. She left him, he was already dressed and ready to leave unlike Morgan who still had damp hair and pyjamas on. She heard him set the alarm before opening the front door and locking it behind him, and she wondered if they would ever get to live out the rest of their lives without the deep-seated fear of being targeted by violent criminals. That feeling was always there, lingering underneath everything they did and was now unfortunately a part of their daily life.

Morgan breezed into the office and smiled to see Cain and Amy already there, working in silence. Amy picked up a sheet of freshly printed A4 paper and waved it in the air. 'These are for you and Prince Charming over there.'

'What is it?'

'A list of the addresses of every rust or orange Vauxhalls that are registered locally. I have another list of ones out of the county. How many do you think there are?'

Morgan closed her eyes. 'Thirty-two.'

'Close, there are eleven but no Mokkas in the county; the closest model is a Crossland and one Corsa. I asked Scotty how big the car was, and he said it wasn't a Corsa, it was a 4x4 type.'

Morgan nodded and took the sheet of paper from Amy. 'Eleven is not as many as I'd feared, but more than I hoped.'

Cain nodded. 'There are only four that are actually local to us, as in, not more than twenty minutes away. Should we start with those first?'

'Can do, what about putting a statement out on the media

asking for a couple that were in Covel Wood car park on the date Scotty saw them, to see if anyone comes forward?'

Amy nodded. 'I'll ask the boss, where is he?'

'Post-mortem.'

'Oh, does that mean I have to ask the big boss?'

'Better had.'

'Me and my big mouth, you just never know what kind of mood he's going to be in and he's not even hormonal.'

'Did anything show up on the ANPR cameras?'

Cain shook his head. 'Ask me if they're working.'

'You are having a laugh?'

'If I was joking, don't you think I'd be smirking just a tiny bit? I'm afraid it's good old-fashioned police work for us today. Apparently, they might still have captured the footage for that day, but until the tech guy fixes the system it's anyone's guess.'

Morgan smiled despite the major inconvenience. She'd still rather be door knocking on enquiries than watching another post-mortem so soon after the last one. 'That's fine, I'll drive, you be my satnav.'

Taking a set of car keys off the whiteboard, Cain followed her out to the car, where she gave him the printout. 'Where are we going first?'

'The Coffee Pot because I cannot stomach any more of Amy's terrible brews, and then the first address is one of those new apartments near to St Marthas that haven't been open long.'

'Perfect, I need to nip in and see Theo. If I buy you coffee and cake, will you go speak to the owner of the first car?'

'Let me see, you're bribing an officer of the law with coffee and cake so you can skive for ten minutes?'

'That's right, I am.'

'Fine by me, I'm always open to a bit of skiving.'

'Don't I know it.'

'Cheeky.'

'It's not really skiving; it's more of a welfare check. Declan said yesterday at the scene he's not doing too good, so I thought I'd pop in and see how he is.'

'Are you going to give him a pep talk, Morgan, see if you can rally him around?'

She looked at him, elbowing him in the ribs. 'Don't be so mean, I can give a motivational talk.'

'Yeah, you could. It would go something along the lines of, I know you got hurt badly, Theo, but did you die?'

Morgan was so horrified she laughed even louder. 'I should make you buy the drinks for that.'

'Bet it would make him smile though. I'll try it on you next time your head's hanging off and see if it makes you feel better.'

She glared at him.

'Maybe not, too far?'

'Far too far, Cain.'

He mimed pulling a zipper across his mouth, and she nodded. Parking outside the café, she left him sitting in silence.

It had snowed in the early hours of the morning, so The Coffee Pot wasn't too busy, and Morgan was out of the door, trudging through the slush on the pavements with the coffees and cake before too long. Cain had put his window down to take the coffees off her and she passed them to him.

'How was Jade?'

'Seemed okay as far as I could tell, she didn't need a pep talk anyway.'

He had the decency to look embarrassed. 'Good, I worry about her. How do you get over losing your only child like that? I don't know if I would be able to carry on.'

There was the sweet Cain, the caring, soft-natured one she loved, who also had the worst sense of humour at times. Jade's teenage daughter Melody had been the sweetest girl, her life taken away by a killer who was now, thanks to Morgan and her team, behind bars awaiting his trial.

'I don't think she has much choice, Cain, the café is her livelihood. If she doesn't work, she earns no money, and besides I think it gives her purpose, a reason to wake up in the morning and get dressed, leave the flat and talk to people.'

'Life is so cruel at times. Hey, did you get Theo a coffee or did you need two?' He was pointing to the third cup in the cardboard tray.

'Yes, I did. I can't exactly turn up empty-handed. Is that okay with you?'

'Of course, I was just checking you hadn't arranged to meet Marc and give one to him. Last thing we need today is him tagging along trying to crack rubbish jokes and make polite conversation, then complain we keep leaving him out.'

'No, we don't, or at least I don't. I already have to put up with you.'

She winked at him and then drove to the tiny parking area outside of St Martha's, hoping she would find somewhere close. There was one other car there, an ancient Volvo that looked as if it belonged in a car museum. There was no snow on top of it, so it hadn't been there overnight.

Cain got out of the car, his boots crunching on the snow that hadn't began to melt, and strolled around it. 'If I was on section I'd be checking those tyres out, the rear ones look a bit worn.'

'But you're not on section so you're not, are you?'

'No, no, no, I am not. We have enough work to do without adding issuing tickets to the list. I'm just saying, it looks like an old banger and not very roadworthy.'

Morgan had never seen the car before but wondered if it belonged to Gordon, the vicar who was standing in for Theo, or maybe one of the older parishioners. She took the coffees and bag of cakes with her, not before Cain had eaten his piece of peppermint crunch in two bites.

'Wait for me here once you've been to the first address, or if you want to come in, do.'

He shook his head. 'Yes, ma'am.' Then drove away laughing, making her smile.

———

Theo opened the door much quicker than she'd expected, and he looked surprised to see her. His face was pale and he had blueish dark circles under his eyes; he looked tired.

'Morgan, how lovely to see you. Come in, I have a visitor I'd like you to meet.'

She realised the Volvo did belong to someone connected to Theo and smiled, glad Cain hadn't started measuring the tread on the tyres, which could have caused some embarrassment.

'I brought you a jar of Ettie's special tea and a coffee. I'm sorry, I didn't know you had company. I can come back later.' She passed the jar and paper coffee cup towards Theo who nodded in appreciation.

'No, don't be daft and besides I've just made John a mug of tea, so he's good. Please tell Ettie thank you, she is such a sweet woman.'

Morgan smiled at him then followed Theo into the living room, where a guy was sitting on the sofa, holding a mug.

He smiled at her. 'Hi.'

'Hello.'

Theo guided Morgan to the armchair opposite. 'John, this is Morgan, a dear friend and a fine member of the local constabulary.'

John's eyes widened at that little statement, and she watched as his eyes fell onto her black Doc Martens, then travelled up her leggings, to her upper body. She'd unzipped her coat, and his eyes lingered on her chest area before making it up to her face. Her hair was in a low ponytail, her eyeliner on point.

'You're a policewoman?' He sounded surprised by this revelation, something that happened an awful lot to her, but she wouldn't conform to what everyone else expected a policewoman to look like.

'I'm a detective, I don't wear a uniform.'

'That's a pity.'

She felt her skin crawl, this guy had to be in his late fifties, with a receding hairline and a combover. Thick wire-rimmed glasses made his small, narrow eyes look as if they wouldn't be out of place on a rat. If she had to pick a serial killer out of a seventies' line-up, he would be the one standing nestled between Dahmer and Nielsen; he gave her the creeps.

Theo intervened. 'No, it really isn't. Morgan is one of the county's top detectives, if not the best. She works very hard to catch criminals. She caught the woman who almost killed me, and I am eternally grateful to you, forever in your debt.'

She smiled at Theo, wondering, how could he tolerate this guy in his house?

'Where are you from, John? Birmingham, I detect a West Midlands accent.'

John nodded. 'I am, but I haven't lived there for some time. I like to move around, currently living in Haworth. Do you know it?'

'Yes, I do. It's a beautiful little village and they have the Brontë sisters' parsonage and museum too.'

John didn't look impressed with her, and Morgan wanted to go, but she made polite conversation for Theo's sake. 'How was the drive down? The roads are not brilliant with this snow.'

John paused before answering. 'I'm staying at a little B&B in Windermere, so thankfully I didn't have too far to travel.'

'That was lucky. I'll leave you to catch up, Theo, and I'll call another time, but I'm glad to see you're feeling a bit better.'

Theo took hold of her arm. 'Please stay, Morgan, you don't have to rush off.'

She wanted to run out of the door, but she wasn't so mean and was about to say yes when her phone began to vibrate in her pocket.

'Oh, that will be Cain. I'm sorry, Theo, we're out on enquiries, so I better go see what he wants.'

Theo looked genuinely sad she was leaving, and she wondered if he felt as uncomfortable as she did around John. He leaned towards her, his lips brushing her cheek, and he pulled her in for a quick hug. 'Be safe, Morgan, thank you for the coffee and cake and thank you for calling.'

When he released her, she glanced at John who was staring at the pair of them intently.

'I will, I'll see you soon. Oh, actually, Ben mentioned you and Declan coming for supper one of the nights. Why don't you ask Declan when he's free and we can sort something out.'

She left without another glance in John's direction, feeling a bit rude. She wasn't normally like this, but she could feel his eyes watching her every move and she didn't like it, didn't like him full stop.

FIFTEEN

Morgan decided to go and pay her friend Brad's grave a visit whilst she was waiting for Cain to come back. It meant she would be out of sight of the vicarage and that was a good thing. Was she being overly sensitive or had her internal radar had a melt down over John? What was his surname? Theo hadn't said and John hadn't given it up either. Then she realised she hadn't told him hers either and took a deep breath. The voice inside her head whispered, *chill, you're stressing over no good reason.*

The grass had a blanket of snow covering it, making the churchyard look serene and beautiful. She kept to the path, or what she thought was the path as there were no footsteps on the grass. She didn't want to be the one to leave prints across everyone's graves and spoil the beauty. It was so still too, she loved how peaceful it was, the sprinkling of snow on the roads had turned to slush, but here it was untouched.

She stared up at the Helvellyn mountain range. It was covered in snow. It looked down onto Rydal Falls and today she felt as if she had been transported to the French Alps, it was so pretty. Then she wondered how many people would try to get up there in treacherous conditions, and the idea of beauty was short-lived at the thought of the traffic accidents and mountain rescue call-outs to ill-equipped walkers.

Brad's grave had a porcelain picture on it, and she stepped onto the grass here to wipe the snow off it so she could see his handsome face. Kissing her frozen fingertips, she pressed them to his forehead and closed her eyes. What would he be doing now? He was an excellent rugby player, would he still be playing professionally or maybe he'd have become a sports teacher or coach. Morgan let out a sigh, thinking it such a waste of his life, he had so much potential and goodness to put out into the world, and yet people like Theo's friend survived.

A horn double beeped, and she realised it was Cain. She whispered bye to Brad and crossed herself for being so mean about Theo's friend next to a church of all places. Passing her adoptive parents' graves, she blew Sylvia and Stan a kiss too. She didn't know the guy and if Theo thought he was okay then he must be; why was she being so judgy over someone she didn't know? That little voice inside her head whispered, *it was the Dahmer glasses, they put you on edge* and Morgan couldn't disagree with it, because they had and the way he'd looked her up and down too.

'Are you mad, what are you doing trudging through the gravestones in this weather, building a snowman?'

She started singing. 'Do you want to build a snowman,' at him, and he rolled his eyes at her.

'Thought I'd say hi to Brad because you took forever.'

'I have been ten minutes tops. I thought you'd be inside with the vicar at least twenty. Why are you out here like a saddo? Did your motivational talk fail miserably and he threw you out, told you to bugger off?'

'No, he didn't. He had a friend there who must be the owner of that.' She pointed to the Volvo and kept her voice low. 'I didn't like him, he was weird.'

'How was he weird? Can I check the tyres now if you know who owns it?'

'No, you cannot, and I don't know, he just gave me the creeps. How did you get on?'

'Old lady, her car and she lives with her husband who is struggling to walk very far. They don't go walking and said she hasn't been to Covel Woods in years.'

'One down, how many to go? Shouldn't Scotty be doing this if he's the one who saw them, be much easier if he was.'

Cain shrugged. 'He wouldn't know them if he fell over them, you know what he's like. He's totally unobservant and if there was a chance he'd have to do some work then he was not looking their way long enough.'

She knew he was right. 'Where next?'

He pointed to the printout on the dashboard. 'You decide.'

Morgan looked at it and chose the one nearest to them. 'We're going to Bowness next, Glebe Road.'

'Good, I like it when it's nice and simple. I don't even need directions.'

'I should hope not, the amount of calls we got there in the summer when we were working on response. Parking issues, domestics, all those tourists love a wild time.'

'I'm glad someone does.'

———

Cain drove them to their next address, which was a detached house. The car of interest was parked on the driveway, and he asked, 'Could this be the one?'

'I hope so, I am not feeling it today. I'm also not feeling my feet; my toes are frozen.'

'No wonder, you jumped into a freezing river yesterday and today you were walking through the snow without a care in the world. Your poor toes will have frostbite. Your turn to do the honours, it will get the circulation moving in your feet and warm them up.'

Morgan couldn't argue with him; it was her turn.

'I'll just turn the heating up and warm myself up a bit more.'

She glared at him, but didn't mean it. Her boots were a bit soggy, and it was her fault.

Opening the gate, she strode up to the house, thinking, at least this driveway had been cleared. The door opened before she could even knock on it.

'Can I help you?'

'Hi, yes, I hope you can. I'm Detective Constable Morgan Brookes from Rydal Falls police and I'm following up on some enquiries.'

The guy opened the door wider. 'Do you want to come inside, it's cold.'

Morgan stepped into the hallway which was toasty warm.

'Thanks, is that your car on the drive?'

'Yes, I don't usually let my neighbours park on it. Why?'

Morgan smiled. 'Sorry, that was a stupid question. Do you ever go walking in Covel Woods or have you been there in the last month?'

'Yes, sometimes.'

Morgan discreetly tucked a hand behind her back and crossed her fingers. 'This is a bit out there, but the last time you were there, were you arguing with a woman in front of the car?'

The guy laughed, but his cheeks were redder than a moment ago. 'I might have been, what is this about because you're right, it's odd. I mean that was about three weeks ago. If this is some kind of concern for welfare or about a domestic then whoever reported it left it a bit late, didn't they? Three weeks is a long time, the woman you're referring to could have been dead all this time.'

Her eyebrow arched; she couldn't help it. Hiding her emotions was not something she was too good at.

The man looked at her. 'You're not laughing. Why are you here again? Because I had a minor argument with a woman I was with? Who reported it after all this time?'

Oh, how she wished she'd let Cain take this one. 'I'm afraid a woman's body was discovered in the river yesterday and yes, I am being serious. An eyewitness came forward to say they saw a couple arguing in the car park, and we are chasing down every possible lead.'

The guy shook his head. 'I need to sit down, come in. Just give me a minute, I feel like my legs are about to give way.'

Morgan followed him into a room with a huge corner sofa and coffee table. There was a wood-burning stove roaring away and she sighed. If she wasn't working this would be a great room to read in. The guy sat down, he pointed to the other end of the sofa, and she did the same.

'Do you know who the victim is?'

She decided honesty was the best policy. 'Not yet. Can I ask who you were arguing with?'

'A woman I know, not very well, though. She comes into the pub I drink in with her friends. I finally, after months of wondering if I should or not, well, I asked her out and suggested a walk through the woods.'

'What's her name?'

'Marie Winterson. Is it her, was it her body?'

'We don't know, can you describe her?'

'Smaller than me, blonde hair, green eyes.'

That wasn't entirely helpful for Morgan. 'Look have you spoken to her since that afternoon?'

He shook his head. 'No, she told me to get lost. I've been off work sick for the last couple of weeks. I pulled my back, and I'm struggling to get in and out of the car, driving a long distance, as it's too painful. I haven't been out much. I'm on strong painkillers which make me feel like shit.'

'Where do you work?'

'I'm an industrial relations manager at BAE in Barrow.'

'What's your name, sorry, I missed it earlier.'

'Anton Highsmith.'

'What did you argue about with Marie?'

'She said it was too cold to walk through the woods, and she thought I was taking her to a pub for a cosy afternoon or back to my place. Which I thought was a bit of a cheek because I didn't want to sleep with her, I was hoping to get to know her that's all. She was a bit forward, I didn't feel that we were the right fit, so we had a minor argument in the car park, got back in the car and I dropped her off outside Costa and left her there.'

Morgan was trying to process everything; she took out her notepad and scribbled it all down.

He waited for her to finish writing. 'Look, I didn't do anything to her, she'll be on CCTV on the main road, or should be. You should be able to see my car driving away after she got out.'

'How did you hurt your back?'

'Picking up milk off the doorstep, twisted the wrong way and something popped.'

She believed him; it wasn't the sort of thing you'd make up.

'Do I need a solicitor?'

'No, not at all. Unless we find identify the body as Marie and find evidence to suggest that you didn't drop Marie off, and you were the last person to see her.'

His eyes filled with tears that he was struggling to hold back. He sniffed and brushed his eyes with his sleeve. 'Look, Morgan, I haven't done anything, I swear to God I've been stuck here and have no idea where she is. If you go to The Angel they will be able to tell you if she's been in or not.'

Morgan felt a little bad. 'I'm not suggesting you have,

Anton, we don't even know who the poor soul is that was recovered yesterday. I'm simply trying to tick off my list the enquiries I have been given. You're not being accused of anything; this is standard procedure. We're looking into anything odd that happened in the vicinity in the last few weeks.'

He nodded. 'Will you go speak to the people at the pub? I don't even know where Marie lives, as she wanted picking up from outside Tesco. They should have CCTV as well of that day.'

'That's good, leave it with me. I just need to speak to Marie and then all this can be put to bed. I'm sure Marie is fine, and this has nothing to do with either of you. It's just unlucky you were spotted arguing by an off-duty officer. Do you have a picture of Marie?'

He pulled out his phone and scrolled through, then passed it to her. She realised it was a screenshot off an Instagram page. Marie was with two friends, and they were laughing at something, a bottle of Prosecco on the table in front of them. She took out her own phone and snapped a picture of his screenshot. She didn't think it was the woman in the river, although they both had blonde hair.

'Thanks that's great, I'll try and get this cleared up, so you don't have to worry.'

He nodded, grimacing as he pulled himself to his feet. 'Thanks, can you let me know when you find her, please, or I'll not be able to sleep tonight.' He rhymed off his phone number, and she wrote it down.

'What's your date of birth, Anton, and how long have you lived here?'

'It's thirtieth of March 1970. I've lived here since my parents died, it was their house. My mum died six years ago.'

'Have you always lived alone? Since your mum passed away?'

'Yeah, unfortunately. I'd like to have settled down, but you know, it wasn't to be. I was hoping Marie might be the one who I could get to know, but it turns out she was a complete bitch.'

This time she did look at him, was he being honest or was he lying through his teeth about everything? The only way to find out was to find Marie and get the ID for the body in the mortuary.

SIXTEEN

Ben had been pleasantly surprised when he'd arrived at the mortuary and Susie, Declan's assistant, hadn't given him the usual third degree over which books he'd been reading. Which made him realise she must do it because of Morgan. He wasn't annoyed with her though because he liked her. She was a genuinely nice person, and when he'd got gowned up and gone into the mortuary, he'd thought he'd repay the favour. Quickly checking on Amazon first, he stepped into the cool, sterile room. Claire and Wendy were both there ready to take the evidence and photos. Declan was fiddling with the radio, going from one station to another then back to the first. Eighties music began to play, and Ben smiled, he loved it. As Whitney Houston blasted about wanting to dance with somebody, Susie made her entrance and Ben took his chance.

'So, what have you been reading this month, Susie?'

All eyes fell on Ben, but he smiled at Susie, taking no notice of them. She grinned at him.

'You got me, hahaha, very good, Ben. I've just started reading *Witchcraft for Wayward Girls* by Grady Hendrix. How about you?'

He nodded. 'I'm not familiar with that one, but I've been really enjoying—' He stopped mid-sentence, what was that bloody book called? He'd forgot it already; he felt his bright idea dropping like a lead ball as he struggled to remember, red cover, eyes through a keyhole. '*The Housemaid's Secret.*' He said it with confidence and was so proud of himself he wanted to pat himself on the back.

Susie nodded. 'Did you read the first one? It was amazing.'

He shook his head. 'I didn't know about the first one, I'll have to check it out.'

'Have you been under a rock this last year, Ben? It's like the hottest book of the year.'

Ben was regretting playing Susie at her own game big time now. Declan, who had been watching the pair of them as if it was some intriguing argument about to kick off on social media, stepped in. 'Well, I am very proud of you both for reading. Perhaps I could get you some little gold stars and hand them out whenever you finish a book. Now, can we focus on the task at hand, please, or would you like to continue and Ben, if I was you, I'd take this get out of jail free card with both hands because you'll never win Susie at a game of what's on your TBR list, ever!'

Ben glanced at Claire and Wendy, who had their arms crossed watching him with amused smiles on their faces. 'I'm ready if you are,' he said to Declan.

'Good, thank the Lord for small mercies.' Declan bent down and, speaking quietly, he introduced himself to the woman lying on the metal table in front of him.

'I am Doctor Declan Donnelly, and I have the task of finding out what happened to you.' He paused. 'Jane, I'm going to call you Jane because at this moment we still don't know who you are, but I promise you we are working on that and as soon as we do, then I'll call you by your real name. Jane, I am so sorry that you are here on my table, but I, we, will take good care of you. I can promise you that.'

The body bag had been removed and after taking her initial measurements and weight, she was X-rayed and then photographed and her clothing carefully handled. She was wearing sodden leggings, a purple jumper, a long-sleeved vest and another vest underneath it. Her shoes were missing along with her coat.

'She was dressed for the cold, yet no shoes or socks, no gloves, no hat or scarf.'

Ben was staring at the hand nearest to him which had hardly any flesh on three of the fingertips. 'What happened to her hand, Declan? Why are only her fingers skeletal? I mean she'd had to have been dead some time for her skin to come off like that, yet her face and rest of her body looks relatively fresh.'

Declan was nodding as he did the external examination, looking for injuries. He stopped at her neck and pointed. 'There is a long purplish bruise on the left side of her neck.' He picked up a ruler and held it against the mark. 'It's seven point two by one point five centimetres in diameter. It looks like it was made by a blunt object, as there are no piercing or stabbing wounds. It looks to me as if it could possibly have been made by the side of a hand.'

Ben nodded. 'Suspicious?'

'Hard to say until I've checked the water content in her lungs. There is something about this that is very unsettling. I have a theory, but I want to wait until I've conducted the rest of the examination before I discuss it.' Declan picked up her hand with the exposed skeletal fingers and shook his head.

'This, none of this makes sense. I'm more than a little confused and that doesn't happen very often.'

Ben was staring at Declan as he studied the fingers on the other hand now.

'Right, well, my initial observations are that this is very

suspicious. There is bruising to the side of her neck, which is consistent with a heavy blow to it. So heavy I think there is the chance it could have rendered her unconscious; it could even have been the cause of death. I will know more when I take a look at the damage it caused internally. But she hasn't been in the water long enough to have caused the skeletal exposure.'

'How can you tell?'

'The skin on her fingers and palms is wrinkled which suggests she's been in the water anything from twelve hours to three days. That isn't enough, there is no bloating, no scalp slippage. For this level of skeletal exposure, I would expect immersion in water for around one to two months. It is possible that her hand got caught in something on the riverbed and the current could have rubbed the fingers against some stones or something, but that wouldn't be this advanced. At this point I have no words. Let's continue and see if these muddied waters run clear.' Declan paused. 'I'm sorry, Jane, there was no pun intended there, you have for the first time in many years caused me some confusion.' He looked around. 'I need to get to work, I need to know what happened just as much as you do. I'm not ignoring you all, but I need to concentrate so forgive my silence whilst I try and figure this out.'

Ben was worried. If Declan was concerned enough that he wouldn't be talking them through what he was doing, this was bad.

SEVENTEEN

The Angel was halfway up a steep hill, the road hadn't been gritted, and Morgan was glad she wasn't driving. Cain didn't seem to mind though and managed to get the car into the car park without too much effort. There was one other car parked, the pub was in darkness and Morgan wondered if it was closed; the roads were icy, it was cold and there was more snow forecast later on, not to mention it was January – and who had money in January to come to the lakes when there wasn't much going on?

'I'll keep the car running for you so it's nice and warm when you get back.'

'I did the last one. I found the guy, you didn't even do anything so it's your turn.'

'Did I navigate the ski run without crashing the car?'

'That's beside the point.'

'Aw, come on, Morgan. I'm likely to break my neck walking to the pub, and you've got sturdy boots on, while I've only got shoes on.'

She shook her head. 'You know you're getting as bad as Des; he used to come up with a million excuses not to do something.'

Cain's mouth fell open in surprise and he unclipped his seat belt and opened the door, getting out of the car. Then he leaned back in. 'I am not anything like Des.'

Morgan got out of the car. If he was going to go arse over tit on the ice, she wanted to watch it – and then she felt bad. Today was the most depressing day she'd had in a long time; it was as if every dead person she knew was coming back to haunt her. She hoped the victims of all the crimes she'd solved didn't start to pay her a visit as well, otherwise she'd end up in a mental health ward.

Cain reached the door to the pub before her and pushed it open with ease, which surprised her, and she followed him inside. There was a roaring fire in the main bar and two guys were sitting in front of it; a golden retriever was at their feet. There was a woman behind the bar, and Morgan smiled at her.

'I thought you might be closed, not a lot of people around.'

'We have B&B guests, so I thought I might as well open up in case any of the locals venture out. What can I get for you?'

'Nothing for us, thanks. We're on enquiries. I'm Detective Constable Morgan Brookes and this is my colleague, Cain Robson.'

The woman looked at Cain, her eyes lingering on him a little longer than was polite, and he smiled at her. A faint redness crept up her cheeks, and Morgan realised she'd been checking him out, which was going to make him unbearable to work with the rest of the day because he'd never shut up about it.

'I'm Sophie Knight, I own the pub with my partner Josh.'

'Do you know Marie Winterson?'

The woman shook her head. 'The name isn't familiar; do you have a photo of her?'

Morgan took out her phone and turned it to show her the picture she'd snapped of the woman Anton had shown her.

'Oh, yes, I do. Sorry, I don't really know anyone's surname just their first names. She comes in all the time with her friends.'

'When was the last time you saw her?'

'Saturday night, she was in here until late, as we had a band on and she loves the live music.'

'You're sure it was Saturday?' asked Cain.

Sophie nodded. 'One hundred per cent. Why, is she in trouble?'

'No, we just wanted to make sure she was okay. We had someone report a concern for welfare for her and we're on enquiries to make sure she's okay. Would you know where she lives?' Morgan had answered before Cain could blurt out too much information.

'You know the row of shops at the bottom of this hill? She lives in one of the flats above them. No idea which one, but I see her quite often when I'm going out.'

'Amazing, thank you, that's very helpful.'

'You're very welcome.'

They left the pub and Cain whispered, 'Well, that gets old Anton off the hook.'

'And Scotty, imagine how bad he'd have felt if the body they pulled out of the water had been the woman he'd seen arguing. Come on, we might as well go speak to her and then she's ticked off our list. I'd walk down but there is no way I'm attempting to get to the bottom of the hill.'

Cain laughed. 'I'd help you up, after I'd taken a couple of photos.'

'Yeah, I bet you would.'

———

He stopped the car at the entrance to the steps that led up to the row of three flats, and Morgan jumped out. 'I'll go.'

She was thankful someone had gritted the path and steps as she climbed up them, she knocked on the first door, but there was no answer; the second door was answered by a guy rubbing his eyes. 'What do you want? I'm on nights. Like did you need to knock as if you're the cops?'

Morgan held up her lanyard with her warrant card on and shrugged. 'Oops, sorry. I am the cops. I'm looking for Marie, does she live with you?'

He shook his head. 'No, she doesn't.' He pointed to the flat where there had been no answer. 'The ice queen lives next door.'

'Oh, she's not in. When did you last see her?'

His turn to shrug. 'Dunno, I don't keep tabs on her. I keep to myself, and I work a lot, so to be honest it was probably weeks ago.'

'Does she live with anyone?'

'No, what is this, fifty questions?' He paused, then smiled. 'Is she in trouble with you guys?' The smirk on his face annoyed the crap out of Morgan.

'No, just checking in on her.' She turned around and left him staring after her for a moment before he slammed the door shut.

As she got back in the car, Cain was grinning at her. 'Your usual charm didn't work then?'

'He was a dick.'

'Does she live there?'

Morgan sighed. 'Yeah, first flat but there was no answer.'

'Don't worry about it, she didn't know she was going to become the main suspect in identifying a dead body, did she? She's probably at work or gone out shopping.'

'I'm not worried, I would have just liked to see her myself in the flesh so I can say for definite she's not the woman in the water.'

He nodded. 'Well, it's clear she isn't the dead body, so I

think that's our mission accomplished. Good work, Brookes. Let's get back to the station.'

Morgan smiled at him. She wondered how the post-mortem was going; it felt strange not attending with Ben, but at least she had done something useful. Now if only they could find out who the woman was, that would be even better.

EIGHTEEN

Declan had finished up the post-mortem, leaving Susie to sew their Jane Doe back together again. They were in his office and Declan passed Ben a mug of coffee, which he was grateful for. He felt as if he'd left his brain at home. Declan sat down, leaning forward on his desk.

'I don't think that the body is fresh.'

Ben shook his head. 'What do you mean?'

'Hear me out, she wasn't in the water long enough for the skin to slough off those fingers. The external and internal bruising on her neck suggests that someone killed her with a single, fatal blow with their hand. I could make out the shape of what looked like a single digit, the end of the fingertip. They could have used an instrument, but the marks suggest to me in all probability it was the side of the hand.'

He ran his fingers along the side of his own hand, making it chop through the air. 'It's rare, not something we see very often, but if you know how to hit someone the correct way you can deliver a fatal blow. Which isn't something everyone knows how to do. I think the killer has a background in martial arts, or the military. To hit with that kind of precision where it only leaves the one bruise and does the job, then I'm telling you it's not your average martial arts enthusiast, no matter how many YouTube videos they watch. If this was their first attempt it would have taken a couple of goes and there would have been more external and internal bruising. I would say you're looking at someone who has been practising for a long time or they are highly trained.'

'Blimey.'

'Yes, blimey. I also think, hear me out, that Jane was killed anything from a week ago to months. I am certain the tissue samples that I've taken will come back positive for ice crystals inside of them, indicating that she was frozen soon after death but not so soon the skin on her hand began to decompose faster than the rest of her body. It's possible that her body well, her hand, was close to a heat source that would have sped up the decomposition on those fingers. Maybe he didn't know what to do with her until he realised her hand was already a mess and decided to freeze her.'

Ben was shaking his head. 'How can you tell that?'

'When a body is frozen rapidly, the size and shape of the ice crystals will differ to if it had been frozen slowly. When blood is frozen some of the red cells can rupture when they're thawed which releases haemoglobin into the plasma. Cellular damage is also an indication of freezing. If the results come back that there is free haemoglobin in the blood then my theory is correct.'

'So, what you're saying is someone killed her with a fatal blow to the neck then froze her body straight away and what, kept it inside a freezer for some time, months, possibly years?'

Declan nodded.

'Wow, that's just... I mean who keeps bodies in their chest freezers? And why now, why take her out now and put her in the river?'

'Your area of expertise, Ben. I give you the answers, you have to solve the puzzle.'

'Yeah, I know that and I'm thinking out loud, but it's the why now that I don't understand. Why dump her body now if he's successfully found somewhere to hide it for so long? And you don't have to answer. I'm trying to get my head around it.'

Declan shrugged. 'Why not, it's winter, the ground is frozen so there is no way to dig a grave, so by putting her in the river it would have washed off any possible transference of DNA, and it gave her time to thaw out nicely so as not to arouse suspicion about the fact that she has been inside someone's deep freezer for an extended period of time.'

Ben's drive from Lancaster back to Rydal Falls passed in a blur. He had no idea if he'd kept to the speed limit because he was too lost in his own thoughts. He went straight to the whiteboard as he shrugged off his coat, hooking it over the back of the nearest chair.

'Listen up, there have been some interesting developments to come out of the post-mortem. I need your full attention, all of you.'

Amy, who had been staring out of the window, turned around and sat up. 'Sorry, boss.'

Cain nodded at Ben. 'Who won the bet?'

At this Morgan wasn't sure if Ben was going to explode or not, but he managed to keep his cool. 'No idea, have we got an ID yet? I need it desperately.'

Nobody answered, and he sighed. 'Declan said her teeth were in a poor condition and it's unlikely she visited a dentist before she died, but you never know. DNA has been sent off and we're waiting on a hit for that.'

'So, how did she die?' Cain was almost bouncing up and down on his chair with the suspense.

'Murder.'

'What, really?'

'No, I'm joking I just wanted to wind you up a little bit, Cain, and see you sweat before you handed your twenty-pound note over.'

Morgan was watching in horror; it wasn't often Ben lost his cool but judging by the red flush creeping up his neck it was going to happen at any moment.

'Knew it.'

'You knew what, exactly?'

Cain's mouth clamped shut and he didn't say another word.

'Have you quite finished, Cain?'

He nodded.

'Good because I'm not in the mood. Jane Doe was killed by a single blow to the neck, most likely the side of someone's hand. That's not the only bit of interesting information. There is a likelihood that she was put inside a freezer very soon after death and kept there for a possible number of months, maybe even years. So, Amy, you need to go back to missing persons reports, say up to ten years to start with.'

Amy gasped but knew better than to answer Ben. He turned his back to them; the room was silent and the noise as he uncapped a marker pen sounded like a gunshot. He didn't look at them, but instead began to use a piece of kitchen roll he'd pulled out of his pocket to clean the board. When it was good enough to write on, he asked, 'Give me a list of reasons why Jane Doe was taken out of the freezer and dumped into the river, and, Cain, please think carefully about it before you open your mouth.'

'They're moving house, or the freezer broke?'

'Maybe they needed room for a turkey?' It was Morgan and Amy who glared at Cain, but he shrugged. 'It's Christmas, I'm being serious.'

Ben let out a long sigh and one hand began to scrub his face, a sign he was getting stressed, and Morgan didn't think what she was about to say was going to improve his mood.

'Maybe you're right, Cain, maybe he was making room in there but not for a turkey or a piece of gammon, what if he needed to make more room for another body.'

Ben turned to look at her and whispered, 'Oh fuck. We also could do with speaking to someone who does martial arts to get their opinion if a single blow to the neck is a viable way to have killed someone.'

'I can sort that out for you, boss. Daisy has been doing karate since she was a kid and helps out at her dad's club when she's not on shift.'

Ben grinned. 'Cain, you're almost forgiven. Can you speak to her for me?'

He nodded, and Morgan looked up at them both.

'Sorry, I think if whoever killed her has got away with it for this long without anyone suspecting, then he's likely to do so again. Maybe he has his sights set on a new victim and needs the space; and if she's been dead a couple of years, is he ready for a new challenge, someone new to make it all seem exciting again and not mundane?'

Amy shivered. 'That's creepy as hell. He kills them, puts them in the freezer and when he's had enough or sees someone he'd rather have in his freezer, he takes her out, drives her to the river and dumps her in it.'

Morgan looked up from the scrap piece of paper she was scribbling on. 'She didn't go in the water at Covel Woods, that's for sure.'

'Why not?'

'How strong is this guy to get a frozen corpse out of the boot of his car or van and carry it a good six or seven-minutes' walking fast to get to the river? Impossible, even if you're the world's strongest man. I mean, come on, a dead body is a dead weight, imagine how heavy a frozen body would be. We need to be looking for the nearest point where the river passes the road, and where someone can pull up next to it to unload them out of the car and drag them in.'

Ben smiled at her. 'Excellent, Morgan, that's good. Get me a map of the area up now, please, Amy. Let's figure out where she went into the water and check for any forensics, tyre treads, etc., that have been left behind.'

All three of them crowded around Amy's desk, and she held up her hands.

'Back up, you're all in my personal space.'

Everyone except Cain stepped back. He pushed her shoulder gently and said, 'Shut up, Amy, don't be a dweeb.'

Before long Amy had Google Maps open and after studying it she pointed to the only place where the river was accessible by a narrow road. 'Under Loughrigg, it's the only place where they could have parked near enough to the river and dragged the body in to dump it. The fast-flowing waters must have carried it along until it got snagged on that fallen tree in Covel Wood.'

Ben kissed the top of her head. 'Amazing. I wonder if we can get a cadaver dog to see if they can pick up the scent and follow a trail. Right, someone make me a coffee whilst I go and tell Marc. He can round up the search team and dog.'

Ben's mood had changed dramatically at the thought of having a possible deposition site for the body. It was a chance in a million, but the killer may have left some forensics behind for them. It was better than the nothing they'd had a few minutes ago. The air in the room was buzzing with the excitement that a break in a case can bring, only Morgan didn't quite feel the same and exchanged a look with Cain that screamed *here we go again*.

The thought of some guy killing someone and then storing

them in his deep freezer made her blood run colder than it had when she'd jumped into the river. She found it disturbing and the thought that he might have taken someone else or have his sights set on another victim wasn't helping her to thaw out any time soon.

NINETEEN

Marc had insisted on a briefing, so an hour later, they waited on him after rounding up as many available officers – and that wasn't many because the roads being so bad there had been several road traffic accidents. Despite the warnings for people not to travel unless they had to, they did, thinking how lovely it would be to get snow pics for Instagram with the whole family without considering how dangerous it was to get to the fells and mountains that were the most picture perfect. Amy, Morgan, Cain and Ben waited for Marc to put in an appearance with a couple of Task Force officers, Daisy and Simon. When he finally walked in, Cain clapped his hands loudly. 'Nice of you to join us, boss.'

Marc ignored him. 'I've been trying to get hold of a cadaver dog. Do you know how many there are in the force?'

Nobody answered, and anyway, he didn't want them to – it was hypothetical. 'Two, and both handlers are on holiday. Who sanctioned for them both to be off at the same time is what I'd like to know, that's just incompetent.'

Ben felt a little deflated at this news. 'Can we get one from Lancs maybe?'

'Already out on a job. I tried. I guess we're just going to have to crack on with it and go search the area ourselves. What are the roads like down there, are they driveable?'

Daisy shrugged. 'If we use a 4x4 we should be okay, but the conditions are not ideal.'

Cain smiled at her. 'Daisy, the boss needs to know if it's possible to kill someone with a karate chop to the neck and I said you'd know.'

Her cheeks turned pink at being the centre of attention, as everyone's eyes were focused on her. 'I, well, yes. Basically the answer is yes it could, but you'd have to know where to strike and how hard. It's not an easy thing to do or at least I imagine that it would take some practice.'

Ben nodded. 'How much practice?'

'A lot, I would think. We always tell students not to aim for the neck area just in case. I suppose a lucky strike could do it, but I mean it would have to be really lucky. I'd say there's more chance of knocking someone out cold than actually killing them. My dad would know more, he's on holiday though. I can message him.'

'Please, would you? I'd appreciate that, thanks, Daisy.' Ben smiled at her.

Marc looked around the room. 'Interesting. Ben, Morgan, Cain, Daisy and Simon can you go down to the possible deposition site and have a look around? Actually, Cain, you'll take up too much room in the car; Ben, do you want to go or stay here?'

'I'll stay; Cain can go.'

Cain tutted. 'Yeah, it's nice and warm here, boss. Look, I don't want to be the one to point out the obvious but what are we looking for in this weather? It's been snowing, the ground is covered, so it's not likely to yield any evidence.'

Ben spoke before Marc could. 'You're looking for fresh tracks near to the riverbank, drag marks, footprints, tyre tracks to see if anyone has been there recently or if she was put in the river before the snow arrived two days ago. I know it's cold and seems pointless, but we have to try, it's what we do, we owe it to her.'

Ben's phone began to vibrate in his pocket, and he excused himself. His animated voice could be heard outside in the corridor, and he walked back in with a smile on his face.

'We have an ID for our Jane Doe. She is or was thirty-six-year-old Martha MacKay, and she was reported missing by her friend in December 2022.'

Morgan gasped. 'She's been missing since then?'

He nodded, and she felt a wave of sadness crash over her for the woman who had been missing for two years.

'Amy, can you get her report up, and print off several copies. I need to speak to whoever is dealing with the case.'

'Where was she from?'

'Birmingham.'

Morgan's insides squeezed a little too tight at the mention of Birmingham. She knew this was clutching at straws, but Theo's creepy friend was from that part of the country. Was it a coincidence that he happened to be visiting Theo and staying in Bowness at the same time Martha's body had been discovered, after going missing in the Birmingham area two years ago? 'Ben, can I have a word.'

All eyes were on Morgan as she stood up and followed Ben out of the room. Behind her, she heard Cain whisper not so subtly, 'What's that about?'

When they were far enough away that the rest of the blue room couldn't hear, Ben asked, 'What's wrong?'

'This is completely out there and most likely too good to be true.'

'But?'

'I have a possible suspect.'

His eyes widened and his lips parted a little. 'You do, how?'

'I called to see Theo earlier like you said I could, and he had a visitor. It was this guy called John. I didn't get his surname, but he was weird.'

'I'm going to need more than him being weird, Morgan.'

'You didn't let me finish. He was like checking me out. It was awful, but that's not just it. He's an old friend of Theo's from the days he worked at the inner-city church in Birmingham.'

Ben's eyes almost popped out of their sockets they widened so much. 'What's he doing here, apart from visiting Theo?'

'I didn't stay long; he gave me the creeps, but he's stopping in Bowness. I don't know how long for or what reason. He may have just come to see Theo, but don't you think it's a little weird how Martha's body has turned up after all this time when she was last seen in Birmingham?'

Ben was nodding. 'We could have two possible suspects.'

'Who's the other?'

He lowered his voice. 'Theo.'

Morgan shook her head. 'No, definitely not.'

'Why, or how can you be so sure? At one point you tried to pin at least three different murders on him. Why have you changed your mind?'

'We know Theo now, he's our friend and he's been through a terrible time. I don't think he brought a frozen body with him when he was sent here and stuck it in a freezer when he's dating Declan and we're two of his closest friends.'

Ben shrugged. 'No, I don't see that either, but we can't dismiss him on those grounds. We're going to have to at least find out if he had any connection with Martha MacKay, or knew of her so we can rule him out. Don't mention this to anyone, okay, this is between you and me.'

'Don't mention John either?'

'No, he's fair game, but let's keep Theo to ourselves until we've cleared up if there's any connections. You know what the gossip merchants are like around here, so let's not ruin his name unless we have to.'

'Declan is going to be so pissed off with the pair of us.'

'Then we won't tell him either. You can go back and speak to Theo on your own. Maybe ask him about John so we can get some background info on him and get him checked out, but whilst you're there see how Theo takes the news.'

'I don't know if I want to.'

'Morgan, I need you to. Look, we both know Theo isn't anything to do with Martha's murder, but because of his connections to Birmingham we have to rule him out. Maybe show him her photo and see if he knows her or looks shocked.'

'Yeah, okay. When should I go speak to him?'

'Now, we need to know about this John guy and find out what he's up to. For once we might be able to bring the killer in before anything else happens. Wouldn't that be something?'

Morgan thought it would be a miracle if it turned out to be John, but she wouldn't bet her life on it, nothing was ever so straightforward.

TWENTY
BEFORE

He hadn't thought about taking another woman until she strolled past him. He was pouring out hot tea from the huge pot into the mismatched porcelain cups sitting on the counter inside of the kitchen's serving hatch. She hadn't glanced his way, but his eyes had found hers and now he knew he was not going to be able to stop what he was going to do. He had to have her; he needed to be able to look at that angelic face whenever he needed.

She was leading a group of college kids around the church. She didn't look much older than them, but she must be if she was their tutor. The woman began to talk to the students, and he listened to her voice, which was as smooth as hell with not one hint of the Birmingham accent. She glanced his way, and he realised he must have been staring too long. He gave her a smile and she smiled back, but quickly turned back to the students. When they left, they would have to walk past his serving hatch, as the other door was shut because there were workmen in that corridor.

After another thirty minutes of the vicar chatting to the

group, they finally began to head back towards the exit. He waited until they were almost at the door before tugging the apron over his head and following them. He just needed to know which college or sixth form they were from, and then he could go on the website and see if she was on there.

As he reached the door, the last of the students boarded the minibus with St Bee's College emblazoned across the side beneath a huge bumblebee. He watched as it drove away, taking her with it, but he knew he'd be seeing her again very soon, and the next time she wouldn't be leaving him ever again.

The next two weeks he'd waited outside of the college, hoping to catch a glimpse of her, and his patience had finally pulled off, when one day he was turning into the car park as she was walking out, her Kate Spade backpack thrown over one shoulder. She had got on the next bus, and he'd had to follow it the best he could. Following a bus around the busy streets was not ideal but four stops later she got off on the corner of a road that had houses on one side and a play park and footie field across the other. He knew that field led to the row of shops and takeaways on the busy high street, and all he had to do was wait for her to use it. He parked up and watched her go into the eighth house along.

It had taken him three weeks of relentless waiting and watching. He knew that she went out for a jog three times a week, always before it got dark. Two weeks running on a Friday night she had cut across the playing field to get to the Chinese takeaway on the high street, which baffled him because she didn't jog in the dark but didn't mind walking across a pitch-black field to pick up her food. People were strange. She was always glued to her phone, and he had no idea what she was doing on there, but it would work to his advantage.

. . .

On the third Friday he made his move.

If she'd paid a little more attention to her surroundings, instead of staring at her phone screen, she might have noticed him following her as she took the path across the playing fields. The sky was dark, with no moon or stars to illuminate the way. Just her tiny little phone torch. She screeched with terror when she looked up to see him standing there watching her. He'd made her jump; in fact, he almost lost his nerve then because the screech was loud, but he laughed, clutching his heart.

'Jesus, you scared the crap out of me. Sorry, I'm looking for my stupid dog; it ran off an hour ago. Have you seen it?'

She shook her head. 'Not as much as you scared me.'

Her voice was silky smooth, her eyes were wide, and she kept her distance from him. She was wary, and he thought she was wise to be wary.

'Sorry, Bertha is a giant pain in the arse. She got out when the Uber Eats driver brought my tea, and I've been looking ever since.'

'I'll help you, maybe she's scared. What kind of dog is she?'

'A pug, chunky little thing, light beige.'

She pointed towards the car park and walked off calling out, 'Bertha, are you there, girl?'

He watched for a moment, wondering if he was being utterly stupid and should forget the whole idea, but he might not ever get another chance and she was too beautiful to let her get away. He couldn't let her walk out of his life like this.

When they were almost at the car park, he made his move whilst they were still cloaked in shadows and struck her across the neck with a blow so forceful it took her to her knees. It didn't kill her though like it had Martha; she was stronger, gasping and gurgling for breath as she clutched at her throat, trying to get up and suck in air so she could scream for help, and this upset him.

He didn't like to see her struggling, or the fear in her eyes. Drawing back his fist, he punched her hard in the temple and as she fell to the floor he lifted his heavy black boots and stamped so hard on her windpipe, he thought he felt the crunch of the bones breaking underneath his foot.

TWENTY-ONE

Morgan was relieved the old Volvo wasn't still parked outside the church. The light was fading fast, leaving the sky a purple, inky blue with a sprinkling of stars across it like some beautiful painting. Declan's car wasn't here either, which was also a blessing because she thought this conversation with Theo was best kept between them for the time being. It was funny how she'd come full circle from being convinced there was something fishy about Theo when he'd first turned up in Rydal Falls. She felt bad having to do this, but far better to come from her than from Cain or Amy.

As her boots crunched through the snow, she paused at the gate, holding the printout with Martha MacKay's mugshot on it, which she folded and tucked into her trouser pocket until the time was right. Theo is gay, she thought, why would he want to kill women and stick them in a freezer? She knew a large proportion of murders against women, especially when committed by a stranger, were sexually charged. She also knew she was right to think he wasn't involved at all; it made no sense.

When he answered the door there was a look of genuine surprise on his face.

'Morgan, wow, twice in one day. To what do I owe this stupendous pleasure?'

She laughed. 'Tell me you've been hanging around with Declan for too long without telling me.'

Theo laughed. 'His sense of humour, huh?'

She nodded, feeling bad that she was about to upset the good mood Theo seemed to be in, but also knowing she had to ask him about Martha because she had nobody else looking out for her – well that wasn't strictly true. Martha had the full devotion of Morgan's team looking out for her now, but still she worried about Theo.

'Can I come in, I'm on enquiries and we're trying to identify the body pulled from the river yesterday. I don't know if Declan mentioned it.'

The door opened wide, and she was glad to get inside out of the cold. 'Has your friend gone?'

'Yes, he left twenty minutes ago. It was so nice to see him and catch up with all the gossip from back home.'

They were back in the kitchen, the heart of the home, and there was a pan of Bolognese sizzling on the cooker.

'That smells good.'

'Does it? I've kind of lost all sense of smell since.' He pointed to his head. 'The doctor said it should come back but I don't know. I thought I'd surprise Declan; two nights on the run I've made tea. I have to admit I've been just lounging around doing nothing except for feeling sorry for myself.'

She knew how that felt, which was the reason she'd always forced herself back to work after she'd been injured, grateful to have something to take her mind off it and a purpose to get dressed and face the world again.

'It's hard, getting back to normal after what you've been through, but it's one of those things. We have no choice but to carry on, otherwise they win. They might not have killed us but if we give up then they may as well have.'

Theo crossed to where she was sitting and hugged her, holding her close, and she held him back and squeezed.

'You are my inspiration, Morgan, thank you for showing and proving to me there is life worth living.'

She smiled at him. 'I'm not sure about that, but you know I'm proud of you, Theo, and so is Declan.'

'What in the name of Mother Mary is going on here? Unhand my man, Morgan, you have your own, that's just greedy.'

Both of them started at Declan's voice. Theo let go of Morgan and Declan roared with laughter. 'Look at you both, you are a couple of cuties.'

Theo glared at him. 'Declan, you scared the shit out of the both of us. Don't you know we were trauma bonding? We could have thrown the teapot at you, or a rolling pin. You shouldn't ever sneak up on us like that.'

Declan held up his hands. 'Sorry, it was a sweet moment, and I am sorry to have spoiled it with my insensitive mouth. I couldn't help myself.'

She shrugged. 'It's okay, I'll get going and see myself out.'

Morgan stood up, unable to mention John or Martha now Declan was here. She didn't think it was fair to Theo.

She had walked towards the door when Theo's voice called, 'Morgan, you've dropped some paper.'

Damn it, a voice inside her head whispered. She turned around to see Theo staring at the picture on the piece of A4 paper.

'Why have you got this in your pocket, Morgan?'

Declan, who had been pulling salad out of the fridge to start chopping it, turned and walked over to where Theo was standing holding the piece of paper, and he peered over his shoulder.

'Is this the Jane Doe from the river? Have you identified her?'

Morgan felt as if her face was going to set on fire, she was so warm. She swallowed and nodded.

Theo was shaking his head. 'Jane, no. This is Martha. What is she doing here? I haven't seen her for years; she used to come to the church for shelter and hot food. Such a nice woman and she rarely used to ask for anything. She'd just come in and sit near the radiator to keep herself warm.'

Declan gave Morgan a look that said *are you telling him or am I?* and she sucked in a deep breath.

'I'm sorry, Theo, the body pulled out of the river yesterday, it was this lady. Martha.'

'Oh.' He turned around and sat down on a chair, his shoulders slumped forwards. He looked devastated. 'I'm confused, why is she here, in the river?'

It was difficult to explain as neither she nor Declan could give him too much information, as they were both sworn under oath not to break confidentiality, but she shared what she could.

'She was murdered, Theo, and whoever did it thought dumping her body into the river would get rid of the evidence.'

He was still clutching the piece of paper, staring down at the grainy photograph. 'Did it?'

'Did it what?' she asked.

'Get rid of the evidence?'

She nodded, now that she had spectacularly ruined his good mood, she had no choice but to question him. 'Yes, unfortunately we think it did. Theo, when was the last time you saw Martha? Do you remember?'

He nodded. 'I do; I remember it well. It was such a bitterly cold night, similar to what tonight is like. I kept the kitchen open as late as I could in the church. I would not see anyone – homeless, runaways, scared, sex workers, drug addicts – out on the street in that bitterly cold weather. I asked the volunteers if they would stay late to help keep them fed, and most of them did. They were very kind; I was lucky that I had so many helpers who all had hearts of gold and wanted to help the less unfortunate as much as I did. I talked to Martha, asked her if she was okay and then I got someone to get her a hot drink and sandwich. She was huddled up near the warmest radiator in the church. I had to go do something else and left her, and when I came back the sandwich and drink were still there on the bench, but there was no sign of Martha. I assumed she'd gone to the toilet or had a call to meet someone. I suspected she was a sex worker, but it was such a horrid night I didn't think she would have gone out to meet a client. I don't think I ever saw her after that, and I didn't think anything of it. The church was busy, always something going on. A lot of the people who used our services were drifters, they'd go from one place to the next looking for handouts and help. It's the nature of living in a busy place like that; people move on all the time. I had no cause for concern. This is just awful, I feel so sad for her. How long has she been dead? God rest her soul.'

There was a look of pain in his eyes that Morgan knew all too well. She had lost so many people in such horrific ways it left a scar on your heart that was hard to ignore.

Declan glanced at her. 'Probably not long after you last saw her.'

Theo sat up straight. His arms crossed. 'What do you mean? How can she have died years ago, and they only just found her body? Was she just a skeleton?'

Declan shook his head. 'It's complicated, Theo, I can't tell you much and you know that I want to, but...'

Theo nodded. 'I know, it's just all a bit of a shock to say the least. Bless her, I always thought she deserved better, deserved more, poor woman.' He stood up. 'I need to go lie down, I don't feel too good, this is a terrible shock.'

He walked to the stairs, leaving Morgan and Declan staring at each other.

When they heard the bathroom door close upstairs, she looked at him. 'I'm so sorry for this.'

He shrugged. 'It's not your fault, it's a mess. I didn't realise you'd identified her.'

'We literally only had confirmation through an hour ago. Is he going to be okay? I called earlier and his friend was here, he was so happy and now I feel terrible to have spoiled it.'

'You didn't spoil anything; it's your job and sometimes you have to ask questions that you'd rather not. Did you come here to ask about the friend?'

She checked to make sure Theo wasn't on the stairs and spoke with a voice barely above a whisper. 'Yes, he was odd, or he was to me, but Theo was happy with him.'

Declan tilted his head. 'Weird how?'

'He kept staring at me, looking me up and down kind of weird. Declan, this is a bit strange, the guy turns up from Birmingham the same time as a body from the same area appears years after she went missing.'

His jaw dropped. 'Oh crap, do you think he has something to do with it?'

'I don't know, probably not but it's a huge coincidence and I'm not too keen on them at the best of times. I don't know anything about him other than his name is John, could you maybe find out more about him and let me know so I can get him checked out, but this is between the pair of us. You can't say anything.'

Declan bit his lip. 'That's a big ask; I don't want to upset Theo.'

'I know, but he could be a person of interest, so we at least need to rule him out.'

'What about Theo, he knew the woman. Is he a person of interest?'

Morgan didn't know what to say as she shook her head, but knew that she didn't look convincing.

'For the love of God, this is not possible. Theo is a good man, and he's been through enough.'

'I know that, we know that. Nobody is saying he did this. I better go so you can go talk to him. Sorry, Declan.'

Declan looked as if he didn't know whether to cry or push her out of the door; instead he opted for pulling her close and giving her a quick hug. 'I'll see if I can find out anything about this John, but I won't lie to him.'

She nodded. 'I wouldn't expect you to, thank you.'

Picking up the sheet of paper with Martha's picture on it, she kept tight hold of it as she made her way back to the car, fuming with herself for making such a mess of everything.

TWENTY-TWO

Amy knocked on Ben's door and he waved her in. She was holding a file in her hand. 'I printed Martha's missing person's report out and her previous intel reports, there are only two. Nothing major, both for shoplifting. She was reported missing by her friend.'

He held out his hand and took the thin sheaf of papers from her. 'Thanks, Amy.' He began reading, and she left him to it.

When he looked at Martha's shoplifting offences he felt his heart tear; both thefts were from a supermarket, first offence was for two tins of powdered baby milk, second for nappies and wipes. Did she leave a young child behind? He never understood companies that wanted to prosecute someone desperate enough to have to steal essentials.

He couldn't find anything that said she had a child or children, but the last sighting of her had been at Bridge Street Church and the name of the detective in charge of her case was a Gulfam Bhatia. It had been a couple of years, and there was a chance Gulfam may have moved on, he might not even be in the force any more. Ben did a search on the internet to see if there had been much uproar about Martha's disappearance. He found a couple of articles and next to one was the photo of a detective who said he was looking into any information with regards to the missing women from that period of time as they are both still active investigations. Gulfam looked very serious and Ben thought that he was probably the perfect detective for this case; he looked as if he cared and wouldn't discriminate against Martha because she was a sex worker.

The next article brought up a picture of another missing woman in her early twenties, a teacher who had gone missing a year later. Gulfam was quoted as saying he didn't think that the cases were connected, but he wouldn't rule anything out. Ben did a search for the missing teacher, Aria Burns, and his entire Google page flooded with pictures of her. He began to read up on her, finding there were far more reports and interviews with friends, family members about Aria's disappearance than there were for Martha's. He stared into her warm, hazelnut eyes and found he agreed with the detective's assumption that there was nothing to connect the women except for the fact that they both went missing from the same area, though the cases were twelve months apart. There was a phone number underneath Gulfam's name, and he didn't think he had much to lose by trying to get hold of him.

The phone rang several times before a voice that was a little short of breath said, *'Bhatia.'*

'Oh, hey. I wasn't expecting you to answer.'

'I very nearly didn't, my friend, I was on my way out of the door. How can I help you?'

'You don't know me, we've never met, but I'm Detective Sergeant Ben Matthews and I'm calling from Cumbria Constabulary. I work in a small town called Rydal Falls.'

'You are right, we have never met but I know of you, or I should say I know of your detective Morgan Brookes. She is very famous in this office; my staff follow her adventures with great anticipation.'

Ben didn't know whether to smile or be horrified to think an inner-city team of detectives kept tabs on what they were doing.

'Morgan is something.'

'Don't be shy, my friend, she is an excellent detective, and we all think they should make a television series about the cases she and you, the whole team, have solved. It's been an intense few years for your department, correct me if I am wrong.'

Ben couldn't correct him because Gulfam was right.

'So, what can I do to help you, Ben, it is an honour to be able to assist you.'

'Do you remember the case of Martha MacKay?'

'Yes, I do. I think about Martha every now and again.'

'Are you aware that a body was found in the River Kent yesterday, of a white female who we have identified as Martha MacKay?'

There was a slight pause, and then, *'Hold on one moment, please.'*

There was the sound of fingertips flying across a keyboard, and Ben realised that Gulfam was logging in. Eventually he spoke.

'I am on my day off; I called in to pick up a gift I left behind yesterday. I had no idea about this, you found Martha and she is dead, yes?'

'Yes.'

'Oh, dear. This was most unexpected today of all days. Do you know her cause of death?'

'She was murdered, killed by a sudden, forceful blow to her neck but here's the strange part. She looked okay, apart from skin slippage on three of her fingers that were skeletonised. I will email you the file with what we have up to now, but the pathologist thinks that she was frozen very soon after death.'

'Frozen?'

'He believes that she was put inside of a freezer and kept

inside of it for years. When did Martha's friend say she went missing? The report is dated the eighteenth of December 2022.'

'That is correct, that is the date I spoke with Melissa. She said that Martha was supposed to look after her baby for her whilst she worked. They took it in turns and Martha never, ever let her down. She didn't turn up for two days and Melissa knew then that something had happened.'

'So, she was missing from the fifteenth of December?'

'Yes, we think so. We only have Melissa's report.'

'Did anyone go speak to the people from the church? Your notes say that's the last place she was seen.'

'Yes, Melissa said that Martha spent time in the church, and I had officers go and speak to as many witnesses as they could find, but there wasn't much to tell. People had seen her on the fifteenth. She had been there, then she left and, unfortunately, she wasn't seen again.'

'Can I ask you about Aria Burns?'

Gulfam let out a long, deep sigh.

'Have you found Aria too? I would feel terrible if both of my missing women turned up in Rydal Falls, but I would not be surprised.'

Ben wanted to laugh at this, but he didn't. Poor Gulfam sounded upset.

'No, Aria hasn't turned up. Could you explain why you didn't consider that Martha's disappearance was connected with Aria's?'

'I spent a long time working on both cases, but there was nothing to connect them, no similarities. They are two very different victim types, they look very different to each other; if there was a similarity between their appearances, their lifestyles, something that connected them, it might have made sense. Martha was a sex worker who drifted from place to place, she was in her thirties and only had Melissa as a friend. No family, no ties to Aria whatsoever.

'Aria was in her early twenties, owned her flat, worked at the college, had a large circle of friends. Aria was of mixed race and Martha white. Aria was very close to her parents, and I talk of her in the past tense because as sad as it is, I believe she is dead. I don't believe she would put her family and friends through this for no good reason, and her bank accounts have never been touched. She wasn't in a relationship, no violent partner, nothing to suggest she was having suicidal thoughts. In fact, the night she went missing she had phoned in and ordered her usual Friday night takeaway at the Chinese. So, we know she was alive at six p.m. when she placed the order for collection at seven.

'Something happened to her in that hour. There is a playing field opposite her flat, neighbours said that she used it frequently to get to the takeaway. Unfortunately, Aria was not reported missing until the next day when she didn't turn up for work and it was well into the afternoon. There was no contact from her which was highly unusual. Her colleagues tried to contact her and failed, her boss went to her flat but there was no answer, so she phoned the police, and we went around to do a welfare check. The downstairs neighbour had a key, her flat was good, nothing to suggest anything had happened inside of it. We had dogs, helicopters, search teams out covering the whole area and playing fields but it had rained badly all night from six forty-five until we got there the next afternoon. There was no evidence, no forensics, no sightings of Aria that night, no reports of anything suspicious. We had nothing to go on.'

'That must have been difficult.'

'It was, but not as difficult as it was for her parents and friends. Look, Ben, I am happy to send all of Aria's information and misper report to you. I must go now; it is my wife's birthday, and she is sitting in the car park waiting for me. If I keep her much longer you may be getting called to come search for me. I am already in trouble for forgetting to bring her gift home with me last night.'

Ben rhymed off his email address and phone number. 'Thank you, Gulfam, if we find anything else I'll be in touch. Have a nice day and tell your wife Happy Birthday from me.'

'*I will tell her the great Ben Matthews, boss of the legendary Morgan Brookes, kept me busy, she will forgive me for that. She is also very interested in the pair of you and the cases you solve.*'

Ben laughed. 'Goodbye, Gulfam.'

'*Goodbye, my friend. Stay safe.*'

The line went dead, and Ben felt as if he'd known the guy forever. He would like to meet Gulfam and buy him a pint. He was as diligent as Ben was and he could think of nothing Gulfam and his team hadn't done in their quest to find what happened to Martha MacKay or Aria Burns; but had they been too quick to write Aria off as dead? What if whoever took Martha had done exactly the same to Aria? Ben wasn't so sure he could assume she was already dead. He believed there was always the slightest chance she might not be, and if that was the case they needed to find her and fast.

TWENTY-THREE

Morgan found Ben sitting in his office, no sign of Cain or Amy. There were no lights on except for the glare from his computer monitor. She walked in and flicked on the lights. He started and shielded his eyes with one hand, before he jumped up and came to see her. 'You scared the shit out of me then.'

'What were you doing?'

'Research.'

'Into what?'

'It's all taken a turn. How did you get on with Theo?'

'That took a turn too.'

Ben sighed. 'Oh, that good, eh? Come on, let's go get a drink, I need something to take the edge off.'

Morgan, who wasn't a big drinker, smiled. 'That is probably the best idea you've had in a long time. Where's Cain and Amy?'

'At the pub, I sent them to get a round in and said I'd wait for you.'

'You could have texted me and gone with them.'

He leaned towards her, pulling her close, his arms wrapping

around her and his lips softly kissing hers. 'I wanted to wait for you, it's been a long day.'

She kissed him back, relishing the intimacy that they rarely shared in work time. Morgan pulled away first. 'Pub, drink, then we can compare the last hour and see whose was worse.'

Ben laughed. 'You're on.'

———

The pub was empty apart from Amy and Cain who had dragged a table in front of the fire and were munching on bags of salt and vinegar crisps. There were five drinks on the table and as Morgan and Ben sat down, before they could even ask, Marc came strolling out of the men's toilet. Cain lowered his voice. 'He caught us on the way out and paid for the drinks and crisps all round.' He pointed to another three bags of crisps.

Ben smiled. 'That's good, we can have a briefing here. There's been a lot of stuff to come out in the past hour.' He waited until Marc sat down. 'Do you want an update now?'

Everyone nodded but before Ben updated them, Morgan wondered if Declan had managed to get any more details about John out of Theo. She took her phone out of her pocket and placed it on the table so she could see if he messaged her. Taking a sip of the glass of rosé with ice she nodded appreciatively at Cain. It tasted so good, it felt as if her shoulders might finally be able to untense and her muscles relax.

Ben lifted the bottle of Stella to his lips and took a long swig.

'I spoke to the detective in charge of the Martha MacKay case, Gulfam. Nice bloke, really helpful. He said that she was last seen at the local church, and it was her friend who reported her missing and that she literally just disappeared off the face of the earth. I believe him when he said they did everything and followed what leads they could. We all know that sex workers don't always get prioritised, especially not in the past. Hopefully we've moved on from that now.' He paused to take a sip of his beer.

Morgan was shaking her head. 'I'd like to think so, but it's dreadful the way those women were brushed under the carpet. How many serial killers chose sex workers for victims because they knew the cops didn't give a crap about them?'

Amy nodded. 'Too many misogynistic bastards running the place who thought they were second-class citizens; it boils my blood just thinking about it all.'

Marc interjected. 'Not on my watch, I mean we don't, as far as I'm aware, have many sex workers, if any, in Rydal Falls because there isn't much call for them around here. Back in Manchester though my department had a busy red-light district, and I made sure we took care of the guys and girls, treating them with as much respect as anyone else and ensuring they didn't have anything to fear when they came forward with information or to make a complaint.'

Everyone stared at him, Morgan couldn't help herself. 'You did?'

He nodded; took a sip of the wine he was drinking. 'My sister.' He paused and she wondered if he was going to clam up, but he put the glass down and continued. 'My sister was a sex worker, up until she was killed.'

Now everyone's mouths were open, shocked at this deeply personal revelation.

'She was older than me, left home when she was fifteen because she argued with our parents all day every day. Especially my dad; he was strict, too strict and spent all of his time at the church instead of at home. When he was home, he just made our lives a misery. Sheryl got mixed up with some older girls who were working and living in the red-light district; the money was good for a fifteen-year-old, it was too tempting, so she did the same. I think it was mainly to piss my dad off, but also because she was this free spirit, and she hated being confined to the life we were living. It was fairly strict, and she couldn't cope with all the rules we had to follow. I missed her so much when she left. At first, she would wait for me on the corner by my school and bring me sweets, comics, things I wasn't allowed at home and I know now that she couldn't have afforded them and must have stolen them, but she did it with love and I still have those comics. They mean the world to me.' He stopped and took another sip of wine.

Morgan couldn't believe he was telling them this, something so personal. 'What happened to Sheryl?'

'She got in the wrong car, with the wrong guy who was drunk, and she was inexperienced, she didn't read the signs, and he sped off with her and crashed into a church of all places. He got out of the car, walking wounded. Sheryl died of internal bleeding, and my parents didn't even let me go and say goodbye to her at the funeral home.'

Morgan reached out and took hold of his hand, squeezing it. 'I'm so sorry, that must have been hard for you.'

He shrugged. 'Terrible, really, I never got to say goodbye and she was the one person in my life who loved me for me, nothing else. She had no expectations of me, I was just the little brother that she adored. I never really forgave my parents for the way they were so strict with her that she felt she had to leave, or for not letting me say goodbye.'

Ben was shaking his head. 'That's so sad.'

Marc blinked his eyes a couple of times. 'It is, but that is why I became a copper in the first place, misguided, idiotic and I had no idea what I was doing but I wanted to help other girls and women in her situation.'

Cain and Amy were at a loss for words for once. Morgan let go of Marc's hand and took a large gulp of wine, never expecting bold, brashy, confident Marc to have a backstory sad enough to make the most hardened of coppers cry.

Marc finished his wine and turned to Ben. 'Sorry for the distraction, so what have we got?'

'I'm sorry about Sheryl, Morgan is right, it is so sad. Are you okay with this?'

Marc nodded. 'I'm good.'

Ben relayed what Gulfam had told him over the phone then added, 'There was another missing girl a year later from the same area, but he didn't believe the cases were connected. The victim types are opposite ends of the spectrum. He's going to send us the files over for both women, just in case.'

Amy asked. 'In case what, she turns up in a river next?'

Morgan nodded. 'I suppose so, a city like Birmingham must have a lot of missing people every year, but I want to play devil's advocate here and assume that she might not be dead. What if whoever took her is keeping her alive, locked away like some kind of pet.'

Morgan thought about Theo's friend John, the thought of him keeping a beautiful young woman captive somewhere gave her full body chills. Not that she had any proof he was a killer, but still the thought was lodged inside her mind and it was a difficult one to shift.

'True, I think it's wise not to assume she's dead, but are we connecting these cases or chasing our tails?' asked Marc.

Morgan's eyebrow arched a little at Marc's response, she hadn't thought he'd agree with her so easily.

'Cain, how did you get on down at the river?'

'There were some tyre tracks near to the riverside in the snow, frozen, and I shit you not it was like an episode of *True Detective*. Wendy video-called some expert who talked her through what to do. I mean it was seriously impressive. She spray-painted the tracks grey, so everything showed up, then took like a million photographs before she took a cast of it. I was seriously impressed, even though it was freezing, and the tracks probably belong to a post van or Asda delivery truck. I mean she pulled a tin of spray paint out of the van as if it's something she always uses.'

'That's amazing, where is Wendy now? We should have invited her for a drink.'

'She went back to continue video-calling the forensic expert. I think she fancied him, she was all smiles and happy when she was talking to him instead of plain angry and snappy.'

Morgan laughed. 'Good for her. That's amazing if the tracks can be connected to a vehicle. I wonder how long it takes for that to come back?'

'The way she was flirting with that guy I'd say a couple of hours max.'

Morgan wondered if the tracks would match an old Volvo. She also kept thinking about the other missing woman. She would do her own research into her disappearance when she got home. There was something niggling away at the back of her mind, and she knew it wouldn't go away until she'd been through everything herself.

TWENTY-FOUR

Ben had insisted they get a Thai takeaway on the way home from the pub, and she didn't argue with him, leaving him dishing it up whilst she had a quick shower. She hadn't been able to get warm all day. She went back down to see him pouring himself a large glass of whisky.

'Want one?'

'No, thanks. That wine was nice enough, but I have a headache.'

They ate in silence, then Ben took himself off to watch TV and she cleared the multitude of plastic containers and washed the plates. When she went into the living room Ben was watching an episode of NoS4R2.

'Hey, I thought we were watching this together, seeing as how I told you about it?'

'Sorry, I needed to take my mind off everything. I can rewind it.'

Morgan leaned down and kissed his head. She wasn't bothered really, she had read the book by Joe Hill and listened to the audio at least three times. It was her favourite Christmas horror story. Charlie Manx was her favourite bad guy after Pennywise the clown. 'It's okay, can you email what the detective sent you about the other missing person's case?'

He looked up at her, then paused the TV. 'What right now?'

'Yes, now.'

'Morgan, you need to switch off, this is a whole lot of complicated and we can focus tomorrow.'

She tilted her head. 'Please, Ben, I need to take a look at it. I'm never going to sleep if I don't. You know I won't be able to just switch off if there is a chance she could still be alive, and I can't stop thinking, what if she is being held hostage somewhere?'

'Christ, okay.'

She already had his work laptop in her hand and passed it to him. He took it off her and hammered his password in so hard she expected the letters on the keyboard to fly off.

'Don't be angry, Ben, I just want to read up on it, that's all. I'd rather take a look now.'

He opened his emails and forwarded the ones from Gulfam to Morgan's email address then snapped his laptop shut. 'I'm not angry with you, I'm tired of us never catching a decent break and I worry about you working too hard.'

She kissed his forehead again. 'Maybe, we should book a holiday and have a proper break.'

He smiled at her. 'What kind of holiday?'

'Well, I'd like a Caribbean poolside villa holiday, but...'

'But what?'

'I'd get bored after a day; can we go to New York or Salem? Somewhere there is loads of history and cool shops. Lots of museums too and good food.'

'I think I'd like that; you choose and get it booked. I'll pay for it; you save the spending money.'

She let out a squeal and grinned at him. 'See, you're not always a moody bugger.'

'Am I always moody? I feel as if lately this job is getting too much, and I take it out on you.'

'You need some more of Ettie's relaxation tea; you ran out ages ago. There is definitely a difference since you stopped drinking it. But to answer your question no, you're not always moody, stressed yes, but I forgive you because I love you and I know that most of the time I'm the cause of the stress.'

He laughed. 'I love you, Brookes, even if you can't sit down and watch the television like a normal person.'

She shook her head. 'Normal is boring, drink your whisky and tell me how good this series is after, if you can remember it.'

She walked out and went into the other living room on the opposite side of the house that they'd turned into a partial home office. This was a huge house for the two of them and she often wondered what it would be like to have a family. Then she thought about Amy who had spent three months solid in the ladies throwing up or constantly peeing and decided that kids were not in the equation just yet, one day maybe, but not now when they were so busy and she needed to see New York and Salem. That was two holidays, at least, for them to enjoy beforehand. As soon as she'd looked at the files, she told herself she would book one of them.

She sat in the soft leather office chair that Ben had spent a small fortune on and sighed. If the chairs at work were like this, she'd have no problem staying late every shift.

When the email opened, she clicked on the attachment and saw the picture of the missing woman, Aria Burns. She was the complete opposite of Martha in both age and looks. Morgan began to read through the report, how had she disappeared off the face of the earth without anyone seeing anything. There were no withdrawals from her bank accounts, her social media accounts hadn't been logged in to since the night before she was reported missing. There was no CCTV footage in the area of her leaving her flat, no doorbell cameras or dashcam footage.

She didn't make it to pick up her takeaway. There was no evidence of a struggle inside her flat, and the police had searched it. CSI had been through it looking for trace evidence and found nothing.

Morgan typed Aria's address into Google Maps and brought up the street map, zooming in on first her flat and then the play area and field opposite. There were lights on the play park, and a couple dotted around the perimeter of the field. Not enough lights for a dark winter night though and that depended on if they even worked. It looked like a nice street, not too dissimilar to the one she and Ben lived on. Next, she did a Google search and brought up all the press releases and news articles. Aria had been big news for the first couple of weeks, slowly fading away to an occasional mention on the anniversary of her disappearance.

What Happened to Aria Burns?

She found a Facebook group and requested to join, not something she would normally do but true crime fans were often good at finding the clues the cops unfortunately some-times missed. It had been a frenzy of posts in the early days, but nobody had posted on there for months. She scrolled through, scanning for anything that might be helpful, but nothing caught her eye.

Eventually she let out a loud yawn and glanced at the time in the corner of the screen. She'd been at this for two hours and found nothing of any use, it was as if Aria had fallen down a dark hole and it just didn't sit right with her, she'd been hoping to find something to give her a lead and the disappointment weighed heavy on her shoulders.

When she went to check on Ben, he was fast asleep on the sofa, the empty whisky glass on the seat next to him and Charlie Manx talking about Christmasland on the television.

She gently shook his shoulder and whispered, 'Are you coming to bed?'

He snorted and turned away, so she threw a blanket over him and turned the TV off, dimming the lights.

Morgan went to bed, but not before checking the burglar alarm was working and the windows and doors were all secured. As she pulled the duvet over her, she thought about Aria Burns, and a voice inside her mind whispered, *I'm going to bring you home one way or the other, Aria, I won't give up.*

TWENTY-FIVE

He had the house to himself, the biggest miracle that had happened to him in a long time. His mother was away for three days. She had moved from Birmingham because she wanted to be near the place she was born, said she would never need to go on holiday ever again.

So, they'd moved and what a job that had been getting a van, then trying to load the freezers into it that were so heavy. But he'd enlisted the help of some teenagers and thrown them a tenner each to load them. Unloading had been a nightmare until the guys who lived across the road had offered to help him and he'd reluctantly accepted. He knew if they dropped one and the catch broke it was game over. His mother had supervised the entire thing, and he'd sweated buckets wondering if his time was up. His mother had gone off on a trip to visit a kirk in Scotland despite her saying she didn't need to holiday now, but if it meant he had three days of privacy then she could go see as many churches as her heart desired. He made sure the house was locked up tight, so nobody could walk in on him, he liked his privacy. He had to make sure his ice angels were all good. He'd got a bit slack with Martha and her hand had started to defrost when there was a power cut. The electric had been off for nine hours, the freezer had turned to mush and the hand that he kept on top of her body had turned to mush too. The rest of her had stayed pretty solid along with her other hand that was tucked underneath her. Now he did maintenance checks on the freezers and his angels whenever his mum was out of the house for more than an hour.

Unlocking the padlock on the garage door, he tucked the key back into his jumper that he wore on an old Doc Marten shoelace he'd fashioned into a necklace. The shoelace had belonged to Martha. It was green, and he'd taken it out of the boots she was wearing before throwing them into the canal. She'd weighed heavier than he'd ever imagined when she'd collapsed – he hadn't meant to kill her. Well, he had, but he didn't think it would work, and if she wasn't such a scrawny little thing it probably wouldn't have. He closed his eyes and watched it happen in slow motion. She had been laughing at him, which had angered him so much he thought about pushing her into the canal, which was so cold she'd have died in minutes, but he had realised that he could keep her for himself, and that temptation had been too much. She'd let out an awful gurgling sound and then nothing. He'd had to prop her up against the wall and hope nobody came jogging down the towpath before he'd moved his car close enough to bundle her body into. It had all gone without the slightest hitch, giving him the sort of confidence he imagined all the great serial killers had after their first kills. He had even driven his mother home from church whilst Martha's warm body had been covered in a blanket in the boot – that had been exhilarating and nerve-wracking, but his mother didn't notice anything was amiss. He'd waited until she'd gone for her bath before backing up the car to the garage door and dragging the body inside.

It made him a little sad that he'd had to get rid of her

recently like he had. He would have liked to keep her forever, but if he bought another freezer, Mother might get suspicious. He told her they were full of maggots and stuff for fishing, and she believed him and told him she did not want to look inside them at any cost. She was the one who'd suggested the padlocks, scared of lifting the wrong lid by mistake, and he'd had to stop himself from telling her maggots were the least of her problems if she looked inside. He hadn't, he'd done what she'd asked like a good boy; he had always been a good boy until things had changed and then he wasn't.

Fiddling with the combination lock he'd managed to open it and push the lid up. Staring up at him, her thick black eyelashes dusted with ice crystals, her lips blue, and her skin as pale as one of the porcelain plates they kept for best. He smiled down at her. She was the complete opposite of Martha, who was much older and had a hard life. You couldn't see her broken neck the way she was positioned now, thankfully, because it had been so ugly. She looked perfect, but he hadn't made that mistake again. There had been a huge uproar over the missing girl and he had never been so scared in his life, posters were everywhere, the entire area and town had been searched. It had rained the night he'd taken her broken body from the field and back to his house, torrential rain which had been a blessing for him, wiping away any possible evidence that could have been left behind. He had stayed inside for days, only going out when he had to take his mother to church and do his weekly volunteer work, or else they would have thought he was acting suspicious, and he hadn't wanted to draw any attention to himself. He had stopped buying the newspaper because he couldn't face looking at the pictures of her that were plastered all over the pages. The headlines... *Someone Knows Something* burned in his brain at night, and he feared that he had gone too far, risked too much. Until the pictures were no longer there every day, the headlines changed and soon she became a distant memory for the people of Birmingham as the next tragedy filled the pages.

It hadn't stopped him though, the fear had only increased his fantasies, and he'd waited patiently until he deemed it safe again to go out hunting for another angel to add to his collection.

TWENTY-SIX

The police station was buzzing with officers who were being directed to go out in pairs by Mads. They knew he hated everyone pairing up unless they were in the van, double crewed answering the emergency calls, but today was different. Ben had looked a little peaky this morning when he'd showered and come down for breakfast, and Morgan worried about the fact that he seemed to be drinking a lot more than when they first met. At work, as they walked towards the spiral staircase, Mads came rushing out of his office, waving frantically at them.

'Missing woman, abducted early this morning around 6.10 from the bus stop on Rydal Road outside of the health centre.'

'Who reported it?'

'A woman was driving past and saw a guy and a woman arguing, she said she slowed down to see if the woman was okay as the guy was really in her face, but he turned around and told her to, "Mind your own fucking business". Said he was terrifying. She drove off and stopped the car around the corner, but not before she saw him dragging the woman into the back of the car.'

Morgan gave an involuntary shiver and looked at Ben.

'Make and model of the car? Registration, description?'

'Orange Vauxhall Mokka possibly, tried to get a registration but said she was so busy looking at the woman and trying to phone us.'

A heaviness filled the pit of her stomach. 'Me and Cain went to speak to a guy, Anton. Oh crap, I've forgotten his surname, it's in my notebook on my desk. He drives a rust-coloured Vauxhall. He's the one Scotty saw arguing with a woman in the car park at Covel Woods, but...'

'But, what?' asked Madds.

'Well, he seemed decent, he said he didn't know the woman that well, it was kind of a first date that went horribly wrong. Then we identified the body, and I dismissed him.'

'Get his address.'

'I know his address, or I know which house it is. He has no previous.'

'But he was on the list to be spoken to?'

She nodded. 'And we spoke to him.'

'We'll go there now, see if the car is there and if he's home. If it is, we'll call for backup. Can you send us some officers to put the door through?'

'Of course, keep me updated, Benno.'

'I will.'

They raced out into the backyard of the station, not bothering to grab a set of van keys because there probably weren't any left at this point. They got in Ben's car, and he sped out of the gates.

'Morgan, did you speak to the woman who he had been arguing with?'

A trickle of cold perspiration ran down the back of her neck. 'No, I already said, because the ID came in for Martha and she clearly wasn't the woman at the scene.'

'No, but she could have been his next victim and now he's gone after another woman.'

Morgan's knuckles were clenched, she wanted to punch something, the window, the dashboard, the fucking guy who had charmed her into believing he was a nice bloke. What was happening to her? She was letting people get to her, she never used to be so gullible.

———

As they arrived at Glebe Road, Morgan was ready to kick Anton's door in herself and drag him out by the scruff of his neck. He'd told her he'd hurt his back, what if he'd hurt it carrying a dead body to and from the boot of his car? Her knuckles clenched even tighter.

'There, that's the house but his car isn't on the drive. You're going to have to go around again, but let me out first and I'll hang around here to wait for you.'

'Where's your radio?'

She pulled the brick out of her coat pocket, and Ben nodded.

'Keep it in your hand and if he turns up you hit that red button, okay? No messing around, Morgan, no heroics, I mean it.'

'Yes, boss.'

She got out of the car and watched as he drove to the end of the road.

It was a very long one-way street and he was going to have to go right around the outskirts of Bowness to get back to the entrance. Depending on traffic it could take him a good five or six minutes. Morgan wasn't waiting around. She walked through the open drive and headed straight to the garage to see if the car was inside. She tried the door, but it was one of those remote-controlled operated ones. Then she walked around the building, where there was a window, but it was frosted glass. Pressing her face against it she tried to peer through the best she could, but there were tins of paint blocking the view. Going back to the front of the house she peered along the street to see if Ben was on his way. He wasn't, then she hammered on the front door. Her girl math told her by the time Anton answered the door Ben should be here, and she wouldn't have wasted precious minutes, even though Ben would kill her if Anton didn't. She wasn't letting another woman get killed for love or money, not on her shift.

There was no answer so this time she drew back her fist and hammered again, so loud a woman in the house next to Anton's opened the door. She looked at Morgan, puzzled as to who she was and why she was hammering so loud this early.

'Can I help you?' Her voice was clipped, curt and she didn't look at all as if she wanted to help her.

'Have you seen Anton this morning? Do you know if he's home?'

'No, I don't know if he's home, but his car isn't there so that would suggest that he's not in.'

'Does he park it in the garage?'

'Sometimes.'

'Was it on the drive the last time you looked?'

The woman stepped out, her floral silk pyjamas flapping in the breeze.

'Look, it's freezing, and he's got a bad back, so he's probably gone to work. If he's working, he would have set off thirty minutes ago. Why are you so desperate to find him?'

A car pulled up and she heard the door slam, relieved that Ben had finally made it. He must have caught the last few words and replied, 'We're police officers, ma'am, and we're trying to locate Anton as a matter of urgency.'

She glared at Morgan, as if she'd insulted her.

'I thought you were his current bit of fluff, not a copper, why didn't you say?'

'We're in a hurry.'

'Try BAE in Barrow, he's probably there.' She paused before asking, 'What has he done? You should tell me if it's anything that puts me in danger.'

'Nothing for you to worry about at this moment. We just want to chat with him, that's all.'

She let out an exasperated, 'Hmph.' Then stepped back inside and slammed the door shut.

Ben whispered, 'Hasn't had her morning coffee yet.'

Which made Morgan grin. There was a video doorbell on Anton's door, and she turned slightly so her back was to it and lifted a finger to shush Ben. She had been so intent on finding Anton she hadn't taken any notice of it. Turning back to it she marched close enough to press the button and spoke: 'Anton, I need a quick word with you. Where are you?'

They waited until an automated voice responded with: *'There's no one home right now.'*

Morgan sighed, it had been worth trying, then followed Ben to his car; her fingertips were numb with cold. It was stupid to come out without a hat or gloves on.

Ben started the engine, and she turned the heating up full, placing her hands on the air vents.

'You know he's probably watched all of that or can do when he's in a position to; he could still be driving. He either knows or he will pretty soon that we're looking for him. He's either going to come to the station to see why or go to ground.'

'Fuck.' Ben slammed a hand against the dashboard. 'Morgan it's too early for this. I have a headache, do you have any painkillers in your bag?'

'No, but I do at the station in my desk.'

'What job does Anton do?'

'He's a manager in BAE Systems in Barrow.'

Ben lifted his radio. 'Control, we have a possible suspect for the abduction, can you add the following details to the log? And also I need a Barrow patrol to go to the following address to see if he's turned up for work.'

Ben gave the control room operator all the details he had. When he paused for a moment, Morgan turned to him.

'We need to go check the car park at Covel Woods and the possible dumping spot along Under Loughrigg.'

'Good call, ring Cain and tell him to take Loughrigg; we'll do Covel Wood car park.'

Morgan phoned Cain whose loud voice told her he was on speakerphone. *'Tell the boss I'm already on the way to the possible dump site.'*

Ben gave her a thumbs up.

'He said you're amazing.'

'What, without opening his mouth? What a guy.'

She couldn't help herself and laughter sputtered out of her mouth. She hung up. 'He is funny though.'

Ben smiled. 'Yes, he is.'

There were officers patrolling all the other areas, and though the ANPR camera on the outskirts of Rydall Falls was still not working, if he drove past any of the others there should be a hit on them to tell them where he was heading. It was really just a matter of time, but time was one thing they were desperately short of.

TWENTY-SEVEN

Covel Wood car park was deserted. Ben turned around, and Cain's voice echoed through Morgan's radio. *'Under Loughrigg is clear.'*

'We should go to the health centre; they must have CCTV footage of the incident if it was at the bus stop outside.'

'Wouldn't a patrol officer already be doing that?'

'I think they're all out searching for an orange car.'

When they reached the health centre, the street had been cordoned off, which was something. Ben parked behind the blue-and-white police tape. 'We can walk up.'

The health centre was open, it was impossible to keep it closed when there were people who needed medical attention, but there was a path across the snow-covered grass that had been taped on either side, with an officer walking any patients and staff who needed to get up there to it without contaminating the scene.

'I'm impressed; they did a good job with that. It's keeping the scene preserved.'

Morgan was impressed too and surprised to hear it had been Scotty's idea. He was the one helping an elderly man up the path, his arm hooked through the man's to keep him steady and safe. Once he'd deposited him in the doorway onto solid ground, he turned to them.

'Good job, Scotty.' Morgan couldn't help herself, praise where it was due, and Ben nodded.

'Yes, good thinking. Do you know if they have CCTV that covers the outside where the abduction happened?'

'Yes, they have, and the practice manager is downloading it for you to view as we speak.'

'Have you already looked at it?'

'No, they're just trying to find the footage. They have a diabetic clinic on this morning they couldn't cancel, so I've been helping – it's been pretty nonstop the last thirty minutes out here.'

'Do you want to come in and look at it, see if it's the same car you saw in the car park?'

'Yeah, I can do but what about my highway to hell?' He pointed to his narrow, now slushy path across the grass.

Morgan smiled at him. 'I'll take over whilst you go and view it.'

A confused-looking woman was being pointed in the direction of the taped-off path, and Morgan strode towards her, leaving Ben and Scotty to go inside. It was so cold her breath fogged up every time she spoke, and she was glad to have a hat and gloves now, after retrieving them off the back seat of Ben's car.

'Yes, what is this? Why can't I use the actual path?'

'I'm afraid it's a crime scene.'

'Is it now. What, did I just get off the bus and walk into a scene from Miss Marple?'

Morgan looked at the woman, who was in her seventies at least, and tried hard not to smile at her. 'Seems like that bus brought you straight to a scene out of an Agatha Christie book, huh? I really am sorry, but we need to keep the path from getting contaminated.'

'You know Agatha Christie?'

Morgan nodded.

'I was wrong about you. I get these impressions in my head of people. I took one look at you and pegged you as a cocky little know-it-all who really knows nothing. I take that back.'

'Thank you, I'm a detective working a serious crime scene who loves to read books.'

The woman shrugged. 'I'm too feisty for my own good, aren't I?'

Morgan shook her head. 'Feisty is good. Do you want to hold my arm and I'll walk you up?'

'The day I need to lean on a detective who is old enough to be my granddaughter to walk up a path, I'm jumping off the bridge, and if I fall on my backside, I give you permission to laugh. Can I ask what's happened? It must be bad for this level of police attendance.'

'There's been an abduction from the bus stop.'

'Oh, that's bad. I hope they find whoever it is.'

She nodded at Morgan and made her way up to the entrance; Morgan pretended not to watch her in case she did slip. She smiled to herself, feisty women were definitely on the uprise, and she was here for that, it was about time.

TWENTY-EIGHT

Ben came out with Scotty, and he waved her over. 'The woman who reported the abduction says the victim was very young. So it can't have been Marie Winterson.'

Morgan squeezed her eyes shut for a moment, hoping that the girl was safe, and this was all some big mistake.

Ben shook her shoulder gently. 'Everything okay?'

She wanted to say yes, everything was fine, but it wasn't, so she shook her head. 'Not really. All of this is making me feel bad we didn't check on Marie Winterson.'

'Do you want to go looking for Marie and we'll see about getting a warrant for Highsmith's house, specifically his garage, sheds and anywhere he can store a freezer big enough to fit a body inside.'

'I need a car.'

Ben handed her the keys to his BMW. 'Be kind to her, she's old. No getting the doors ripped off her, please.'

'As if, that was not my fault. Not one little bit.'

He winked at her.

'How are you going to get back to the station if I have your car?'

'Scotty is going to lend me the van; even better, Scotty is going to drive me back because the cavalry has arrived.'

Morgan frowned at him, no clue as to what he was talking about until she heard doors slam a little further down the street and turned to see four PCSOs walking towards them. Ben was smiling. 'The experts are here now; they'll have this place sorted and organised in minutes. We'll go through the CCTV and hope we can ID this man, or the victim.'

'Catch you later.' Morgan was already walking away from him towards his car. 'Hey, ladies, it's freezing. Have you got gloves and thermal underwear on?'

Sam and Tina nodded. 'Always come well prepared, we never know when you guys are going to need us to stand around for hours getting hypothermia.' She lifted her trouser leg to show Morgan a pair of ultra thick thermal socks. 'I never work a cold day without these on, my toes can't take it anymore.'

'I don't blame you; I've got two pairs of socks on, and my toes are numb. See you both later. If you need a hot drink or anything give me a shout, okay?'

'Thanks, Morgan.'

Sam smiled at her as she headed towards Ben's car. She was going back to Marie's flat and then if she got no reply, she was going to have to start going through her social media accounts to find out where she worked or who her friends were. She had an intense feeling that it was a mistake not to have found Marie yet. A sense that perhaps she was missing. She should have clarified she was alive and well, then she wouldn't have this churning dread in her stomach.

———

Morgan hammered on the flat door, but the noise seemed to echo around the inside of it. Pressing her ear to the door she got the impression that the flat was empty. It sounded hollow inside, it also sounded silent, no radio, TV, no background noise at all like there was when you were home. She was beginning to get worried for the woman and hoped that Anton Highsmith hadn't done anything to her.

The nosy neighbour opened his door. 'You again.'

'Hi, yes, it's me. Detective Brookes. Have you seen Marie since I was last here?'

He shook his head. 'Nope.'

'Is she normally not home like this?'

'It's daytime, she works. Why don't you call after tea when she might be home?'

Morgan felt a little foolish that she hadn't factored in that she would be out of the house because of her job. As much as she hated to ask, she had nothing to lose. 'Do you know where she works?' She crossed her fingers, needing desperately to catch some kind of break.

He paused as if considering if he should tell her this information. 'Tesco.'

'Which Tesco?'

She hoped he was going to say the one around the corner.

'Down the street.'

Morgan felt her shoulders relax a little. 'Thanks.'

He nodded and went back inside of his flat, and she began the slow walk down the steep hill to get to Tesco, thanking whoever had the foresight to get out early and grit the pavements, otherwise she'd have gone arse over tit the entire length of the street, landing directly outside the sliding doors to the supermarket.

It was dead inside, and she went straight to the nearest woman wearing a uniform who was stacking a shelf.

'Hi, I'm looking for Marie Winterson.'

Her blonde hair in a ponytail she looked familiar, and Morgan was relieved. The woman eyed her suspiciously.

'That's me.'

'Phew, am I glad to see you.'

'Pardon me, but why?'

A family came through the doors, and Morgan said, 'Do you have somewhere we can talk a bit more privately?'

'I'm sorry, but who are you?'

'Sorry, I was so relieved to see you're okay. I'm Detective Constable Morgan Brookes; I wanted to speak to you about Anton Highsmith.'

Marie rolled her eyes. 'Oh, right. I told my friends he was weird, what's he done?'

She led Morgan through a set of double doors out into the stockroom; it was freezing out there.

'Nothing that we know of, but a concern for welfare came in about you. Someone reported that you were arguing with him in the car park at Covel Woods a few weeks ago, and we wanted to make sure you are okay.'

Marie squinted her eyes. 'Is it anything to do with the body you pulled out of the water? Did you think it was me?'

Morgan nodded, and Marie cupped a hand to her mouth.

'Oh, wow. I'm glad it wasn't me.'

'So, am I or we wouldn't be here now.' Morgan smiled a little at her.

'He is good-looking, lives on his own, nice house, offered to take me out and I said to my mates he better take me somewhere nice, you know. Posh restaurant, pub, I mean we live in the Lake District, he's spoiled for choice, and he took me for a walk in the woods like some bloody serial killer. I told him no; well, I was a bit rude to him actually and I do feel a bit bad about that, but you read about all these women who go missing, don't you, in the woods and I got a bit freaked out, that's all.'

'Did he do or say anything weird to you, was he violent towards you?'

She shook her head. 'No, God nothing like that apart from

let's go for a nice country walk, the route is flat so it's not too hard. Is that weird enough?'

Morgan had to cup a hand over her mouth and pretend to cough to stifle the laughter that was threatening to erupt.

'You don't like walking?'

'It's winter, it's too cold and my idea of a good time is not walking through some muddy wood and freezing my tits off. I mean, come on, would you want to do that, seriously?'

Morgan did laugh, she couldn't help herself, and Marie let out a small giggle too.

'I mean, I'm a chunk who prefers a bottle of fizz and fish and chips, sod all that walking unless it's walking from pub to pub or to the chippy. I'm not interested.'

Morgan had an irrational urge to lean forward and high five Marie but didn't.

'I don't blame you. I'm glad you're okay, thank you for chatting to me.'

'I feel so bad for whoever was pulled out of the river. Do you think it was Anton? Could he have done it and then done the same to me? One quick shove on the slippery banks and whoosh, in I'd have gone like a beached whale and that could be my body you're dragging out of there.'

'We don't have any evidence to say it was him, but you were right to say no. If you think of anything that might be relevant you can ring me on this number.' She pulled a card out of her pocket and passed it to Marie, who tucked it into hers.

'Thanks, but there's nothing else really. He drove me straight back and dropped me off next door at Costa, no funny business.'

'I'm glad, take care, Marie.'

She left Marie who had already waved over another worker, no doubt to fill her in on what Morgan had been asking her.

As she walked back up the hill she phoned Ben.

'Marie Winterson is alive and well, works in Tesco Express and had no complaints about Highsmith.'

'Well, that's something I suppose.'

'How are you getting on?'

'Just waiting on the warrant to get signed. Do you want to head back here? The CCTV was very poor quality, hard to distinguish anything other than a man and woman arguing before she's bundled into the car.'

'On my way.'

'Why are you out of breath, have you been running, Morgan?'

She laughed. 'It's a steep hill from Tesco to the rear of her flat where I left your car.' She hung up and thought that she agreed with Marie: she'd much rather be sitting in a cosy pub than out walking around and freezing her tits off.

TWENTY-NINE

Theo was on his own. As far as he knew he wasn't getting any visitors except for maybe Gordon who kept popping in every couple of days, which was good of him. He got the feeling that Gordon was trying to gauge whether Theo was going back to work sometime soon, and he knew that he should. He was going out of his mind staring out of the bedroom window every day at the entrance where he was attacked.

He watched as a rusty old Volvo parked outside the church and wondered who it was. Then he saw John get out and for a moment debated on moving away from the window so he couldn't see him. It had been fun to catch up with him yesterday, but he really was too tired today to make polite conversation. So, he froze and hoped he wouldn't look up to where he was sitting, and wouldn't you just know it, John did indeed stare up at the window he was sitting in, smiled and waved. Theo groaned inwardly, a loud one, but waved back and forced himself to smile at the man. Pushing himself out of the chair he went down the stairs and opened the front door to let him inside.

'Theo, how are you today?'

'I'm good, what brings you here?'

'I didn't want to leave without saying goodbye. It was so good talking to you yesterday I'd forgot how much we got along. You are probably one of my dearest friends, I don't have many.'

'Come in, let me get you a coffee before you set off then, and I think there are still some cakes left.'

John followed him down to the kitchen, and he wondered if he should have thrown himself onto the bedroom floor when he'd had the chance. John took a seat and let Theo make him a coffee. There were two cakes left, and he put one on a plate to offer to John, the other he was saving for Declan. John ate the cake off the plate, and when Theo was brewing the coffee he also helped himself to the other one. He didn't notice until he turned around and looked at the plate with two empty wrappers. John was licking his fingers.

'They were so good; you could bake professionally.'

'Oh, I was saving that one.'

'I'm sorry, I'm a greedy git when it comes to cake. I have no self-control. Sorry.'

At that moment Theo wanted to tell him to get out. He couldn't be bothered with him today, but he just couldn't do it. Yesterday had been nice, reminiscing about the good times they'd had at the church and catching up on what everyone was up to, but he was so exhausted today and would prefer to be alone.

'So, Theo, just how well do you know that very attractive woman who came here yesterday? Did you see those legs and that tight shirt? It's enough to make any man run to the bathroom.'

Theo slammed down the mug he was holding, hot coffee sloshing all over the counter.

'Please, John, don't talk about my friend that way. I don't like it, and she deserves more respect than that.' Theo tried to remember if John had always been this way about women. He couldn't say that they had ever been in the situation where these kinds of comments had been mentioned; had John always been so misogynistic and he just hadn't noticed?

'Oh, I'm sorry, Father. I forget that you don't really like women so you wouldn't appreciate that kind of thing.'

Theo turned around and set the mug in front of John with a thump, sending more coffee spilling over the tabletop. 'The fact that I am gay has nothing to do with the way you talk about my friends, John. You shouldn't talk about any woman like that, it's very disrespectful.'

John stared at him. 'Sorry, did I upset you? I wondered if she had a fella she was serious about, you know, or do you think she would be okay if I asked her out?'

Theo's mouth was open, and he couldn't help it. He lifted his coffee mug to his lips and took a sip, trying to gather his thoughts together. John was staring at him expectantly.

'I'm at a loss for words, John. First of all, I think you should know that Morgan is in a loving relationship with her partner and has been for a few years. She isn't available or looking to date anyone.' He had to stop himself from saying *and she definitely wouldn't go out with you.*

John looked surprised. 'She is, oh of course she is. I mean why wouldn't she be, sorry that was stupid of me.'

Theo shrugged. 'Not stupid, you felt attracted to her so there is nothing wrong with asking.'

John nodded. 'Never mind. So, when are you going back to work? It can't be good for you moping around the house all day staring at the church. Wouldn't you be better to get on with it, you know, face your fears?'

Declan walked in and stared with one eyebrow arched at the man sitting opposite Theo.

Theo was surprised to see him. 'Declan, what are you doing back?'

Declan was staring at the empty cake wrappers on the table. 'I forgot my cake.'

Theo looked mortified, but John didn't seem to care at all, then Declan winked at Theo who felt his horror dissipate.

'Declan, this is John, from my old church.'

Declan nodded. 'Theo, I need you to help me out with something. I'm sorry, John, but he's going to be busy, so there isn't much point in you hanging around.'

John looked shocked that he'd just been told it was time to leave, but Theo could have kissed Declan.

John stood up. 'Well, it was good to see you, Theo. Take care.'

'You too, John, safe travels.'

'I'll see you out.' Declan almost chased him out of the room and towards the front door. He didn't say goodbye to the guy and shut the door behind him.

Theo had followed them. 'Thank the Lord for small mercies,' he whispered.

'Theo, he was repulsive, why didn't you tell him to bugger off?'

He shrugged. 'I don't know, he was different yesterday. Then he changed after Morgan called and...'

'Well, thank Mother Mary of Jesus I forgot my phone, or you could have been stuck with him forever. I overheard you telling him he'd eaten my cake and that was enough for me.'

'I thought you came back for your cake?'

'I was teasing.' Declan leaned forward and kissed Theo's cheek. 'What are you doing now I've liberated you? I mean, I won't stop you if you want to bake more cakes, seeing as how your friend ate the last one.'

Theo smiled at him. 'I might, but I also think I'll have a walk over to the church, maybe go and tell Gordon I'm ready to get back to work.'

Declan's eyes sparkled and he blinked a couple of times. 'You're ready to go back? Do you want me to come with you?'

'No, I'm fine. I need to do this in my own time, and besides you're a very busy man; I don't want to hold you up. I need to get on with it. I couldn't stop thinking about Morgan after she left yesterday. She has literally been attacked more times than I can count, she's been in fights, saved lives, almost lost her life yet she still goes back to the same job and does it all over again. She is so selfless and puts everyone before her own needs. She wouldn't be moping around feeling sorry for herself, and now I think about how I've been behaving, I feel quite the idiot.'

Declan nodded. 'She's been through a lot, but so have you and I'm proud of you, Theo. I'll tell you something though.'

'What?'

'Not as proud as Gordon will be if those women haven't sorted out the calendar photos.'

Theo groaned, then laughed. 'Are you trying to stop me from going back?'

'Not at all, I think you will have plenty to keep your mind occupied when you have to decide which ones make the cut for the calendar, then once you've decided you will have the wrath of the unpicked women to contend with. Plenty to keep your mind busy.'

Declan ran upstairs to retrieve his phone, and when he came down with it he shouted to Theo, 'Lock the door behind you if you go out; actually, lock it after me if you don't. Or you might get stuck with another person you can't be bothered talking to and I won't be coming back to rescue you for a second time.'

Then he was out of the door and rushing back towards his car.

Theo did lock the door behind him. He was going to get dressed, put his black shirt and dog collar on to prove he was back in the game, then he was going to tell Gordon he was relieved of all calendar duties.

THIRTY

'There was no sign of Anton Highsmith at his workplace. Barrow officers went straight there and according to them, after some lengthy internal phone conversations, they were able to confirm that he was still signed off on the sick,' Ben told the faces of everyone who was seated and standing in the blue room that were staring at him.

Cain's hand lifted. 'What are we doing, staking out his house?'

'Better than that, you got the warrant signed, did you not?'

'Yes.'

'Well then we're going to put his door through and then we're going to search his garage or anywhere else that he might have a chest freezer big enough to store a body inside. Have we got any door entry trained officers here before I have to call in Task Force?'

Cain's hand went up again.

'Sorry, Cain, I wanted you on the initial search team with me and Morgan, but if there's no one available can you go get your gear on?'

'No worries, where are Task Force though?'

'Drug warrant in Kendal. Al said as soon as he can spare someone, he'll send them our way.'

Amy smiled at him. 'You like dressing up like Robocop, Cain, don't pretend that you don't.'

He blew her a kiss and left the room.

Wendy came rushing in, waving a sheet of paper in Ben's direction.

'I have some forensics back from the tyre tread. There were some flakes of brown paint in the impression before I sprayed it that I managed to retrieve, combined with the results from the tread. The car you're looking for is a Vauxhall Zafira; it has to be an older model if the paint is chipping off.'

Ben let out a sigh. 'That's great, thanks, Wendy. We've got a warrant for a guy who drives a Vauxhall but not a Zafira.'

'He might have two cars, Ben, it's not unheard of. All I'm saying is that if you find another body or even if the missing woman is alive, if she's got any matching paint flakes on her then you know he's your guy one hundred per cent.'

'Amazing, thank you.' Ben looked to Marc. 'Now what, boss?'

'We continue with the plan. Who's to say Highsmith doesn't have access to two cars, there is no telling what he has in the garage.'

There were pictures of Highsmith's house zoomed in off Google Maps on the smartboard.

Morgan wasn't convinced but kept quiet until Ben said, 'Morgan, I want you to stay here and hold the fort, keep us updated if there are any sightings of Highsmith.'

Usually she would argue, but she had an idea in the back of her mind that had been there since she'd been searching for information on Aria Burns. She nodded and stood up.

'I have some stuff I need to do; I'll keep in touch if we get anything.' She left them to it. She wanted to go through the missing person's file on Aria. It was in her opinion far too much of a coincidence that two women in the same area had disappeared off the face of the earth with nothing to say what had happened despite there being a big difference in the victim type.

In the office she stared at the whiteboard where Ben had scribbled Gulfam Bhatia's phone number. She had nothing to lose so she phoned it.

'*Bhatia.*'

'Oh, hi, this is Detective Morgan Brookes from—'

'*Really, you are the great Morgan Brookes, calling me?*'

A look of confusion crossed her face. 'I'm sorry do I know you?'

Gulfam let out a snort of laughter.

'*No, I am sorry, Morgan, I don't believe you do. Although as I told your boss yesterday, I know of you, we all do, and it is a great honour to speak with you.*'

This totally threw her, and she felt her cheeks begin to burn. 'It is? Actually the honour is all mine, Gulfam. I have a favour to ask regarding the Aria Burns case.'

'*Anything you need, Morgan; I am very honoured you are interested in this missing persons case. It is very sad we don't know what happened to Aria. How can I help you?*'

'It is awful. Ben mentioned you sent him the files and I've taken a look at them, but I wondered, do you still have the house-to-house enquiries written down somewhere?'

'*We should do; I keep everything pertinent to each investigation.*'

'Are they already in the file you sent over? I must have missed them.' She had been reading the file last night with her eyelids drooping. She'd been so exhausted and could have missed them.

'*The results were that house to house was a negative. I don't believe anyone bothered to scan the printed forms onto the system. I would have to search through the filing cabinets to see if they are still there. They should be because it's an ongoing investigation. Can I take your number and call you back?'*

'Yes, of course.' She gave her telephone number, and he wished her a pleasant day. She smiled to herself. He was a lovely man and she hoped they still had those enquiries. Someone must have noticed something going on.

In the meantime, she opened the file that Ben had forwarded on to her and sent the entire thing to the printer. It was easier to digest when it was printed out rather than on a computer screen.

Amy came in, sat down and gave the biggest sigh.

'Are you okay? How's it going?'

Morgan pointed to Amy's very pregnant belly.

'I'm just so tired all the time and I feel so bad still living in Cain's house, not that he's ever there, but you know I feel like I'm putting on him; and I am sick to death of peeing. I spend more time in the toilet than I do at this desk.'

'You know he loves that you're living there so I wouldn't be worrying about that.'

'He does? I was worried I'd be getting on his nerves by now. I can't find anywhere suitable or in my price range and it's so depressing. I wanted to be settled in a little flat somewhere and there's nothing out there.'

'When are you due?'

'I've got eleven weeks to go.'

'Are you nervous, I think I'd be terrified.'

Amy shrugged. 'Nervous and not really looking forward to lying there giving birth with Cain standing next to me, but he's been so good to me and he's very excited about the birth, so I don't feel as if I can say no.'

'He wouldn't mind if you'd rather he wasn't there.'

'I know, but he's better than nobody. I don't know how women do it when they're alone and have nobody to scream at.'

Morgan smiled at her. 'I'd be there if you'd rather a woman.'

'Thanks, Morgan, but I don't think Cain would forgive me. Although he may chicken out yet. He might be all talk and when it comes down to it, pass out and miss the actual birth.'

Morgan didn't think he would. He had sounded really excited the last time he'd talked about it.

Amy stood up. 'I'm going to the loo for the twelfth time this hour, do you want a brew?'

They both laughed and Morgan nodded. 'That was poetry of the highest degree, I'd love a coffee if it's not much trouble.'

Amy left her and Morgan felt sorry for her, but Cain wouldn't see Amy out on the street. He'd mentioned renting his house out to Amy, but must have forgotten to actually tell Amy that was a possibility. She better remind him later when he came back. She went to grab the files from the printer. Her desk was cluttered, but Des's old desk was still empty, so she sat there and spread the sheets out, sorting them into piles, incident report in one, witness statements in another.

Amy brought her a mug of coffee and put it on the desk. 'Anything interesting?'

'I'm sure both missing women are connected. It's not right that both of them vanished and have been gone for such a long time without a trace. If the same guy who killed Martha took Aria, then it's a possibility she's in his freezer too. Who knows how many other bodies he has stored in them? However, I don't want to rule out the chance she could be alive. He could be keeping her hostage.' Morgan sighed, there were a lot of *what ifs* but as long as it was a possibility she would never give up hope.

Amy shuddered. 'It freaks me out, imagine dying and then being shoved into a freezer. Brrrr. It's awful. Look, Morgan, I feel terrible. I can't shift this headache I've had all day, and I asked Marc if I could finish early. Are you okay with that, or do you need a hand?'

'No, you get yourself home, Amy. Do you need a lift?'

'I'm good, the fresh air will help my head.'

'If you ever need anything ring me or message. I can go shopping or pick stuff up for you, it's no bother at all. Even if you just want someone to vent off about stuff, I'm always here.'

Amy smiled at her. 'I might just do that, the shopping I mean. Cain is rubbish at buying junk food. He buys the crap he wants to eat and thank you, good luck.'

She pulled her coat, scarf and gloves on then walked out of the office, leaving Morgan alone, which she didn't mind because she could more easily concentrate in the quiet office. Picking up the witness statements, there weren't many: her parents, sister, the guy in the flat above Aria's and the two next-door neighbours. As she read through them, she felt sad that this bright young woman had vanished without a trace and was most likely dead. The last witness statement was four lines on a single sheet of paper, and it had been taken from one of the neighbours.

Sheila Grant had heard a woman calling out and shouting for a dog on the playing fields sometime between six and eight p.m. on the night Aria went missing. Morgan thought about what she had said, as there were no follow-up statements: who was the woman looking for her dog that Sheila Grant heard? There was a chance this woman might have witnessed something, and she wondered if Gulfam's team had traced her and spoken to her. Just then, the phone on her desk began to ring and she rushed over to pick it up.

'Brookes.'

'*Hello, Morgan, it's Gulfam. I have some sad news for you. I have not been able to locate the original house-to-house documents.*'

'That's okay, Gulfam, it was a big ask. I doubt many of ours have been kept from that far back. Thank you for looking.'

'*My pleasure.*'

'I was reading through the press releases, appeals and statements one stood out to me, Sheila Grant's; she said she heard a girl calling out for a dog. Did anyone manage to locate her and speak to her?'

'I'm afraid not, she never came forward despite several pleas through the press and social media. We ruled her out as being a witness because if she had seen anything untoward happening, I like to think she would have broken her silence.'

'Do you think there is a chance it could have been Aria?'

'What? Calling out for a dog? I do not think so, she did not own a dog or ever walk one that we are aware of.'

Morgan paused before asking, 'Did the neighbour say if she recognised the voice or ever heard the woman calling out before or after?'

'No, she said she was closing her curtains when she heard a female voice calling out and assumed whoever it was had lost their dog.'

'What if someone lured Aria to their car by pretending they were looking for a dog? And it was Aria calling out for the dog. It would explain why nobody ever came forward to tell you it was them. There is nothing for anyone to be scared about by coming forward if they had genuinely lost their dog.'

'Oh, dear. We didn't take that into consideration, not one little bit. Leave this with me, Morgan, and I will go and see if the neighbour is still there. Perhaps she can shed a little more light on the incident in question. Goodbye for now, Morgan.'

'Bye, Gulfam.'

She put the receiver down. She had that fizzing sensation in her stomach that she sometimes got when she was onto something. If the woman calling for a dog was Aria, that meant whoever took her had used that scenario to lure her towards him or to his vehicle. Had Martha been lured the same way?

Morgan thought about Theo's church and John, he was creepy. Theo said himself that Martha was a frequent visitor to the soup kitchen. John worked there, and he drove a Volvo which had the longest boot she knew of and would fit a body inside of it quite nicely. A cold shiver ran the full length of her spine. Was he their killer? She needed to know more about him, where he lived, did he live in close proximity to where Aria was taken from? Did she know him? If she recognised him, she wouldn't have felt threatened by him. The fact that he was here when Martha's body had been discovered was the main strike against him.

She took out her phone to ring Theo, but there was no reply. She was going to have to talk to him about his friend. Warn him that he might be harbouring a killer, and it made her feel bad to be the one to tell him this, but Theo had been through enough, and he didn't need the additional stress.

Given what she'd discovered, she thought Anton Highsmith was more than likely a false lead, although there was the report of the woman he had supposedly abducted. She was going to Theo's, she decided; Ben was capable of handling Highsmith, and if she was right, at least she would be able to give him an alternative suspect.

THIRTY-ONE

Amy had forgotten how treacherous the pavements were, and it was so bloody cold, she wished she'd taken Morgan up on her offer of a lift, but she was halfway back to Cain's and there was no way she was turning back and walking to the station. She may as well carry on despite the burning sensation in her calves. At least she was bundled up in her padded winter coat and warm enough. A car drove past her, churning up the snow that had turned to slush at the side of the road, and she felt it splatter up her leggings, soaking her with freezing icy water.

'Christ,' she swore, and the car stopped abruptly. A man got out of it and rushed towards her. 'I'm so sorry, did I get you wet? I wasn't paying attention and drove a little too near to the kerb.'

She glared at him then realised she recognised him and stopped. 'It's okay, you just shocked me, that's all. I'm fine, just a little soggy.'

'Are you going far? I can give you a lift; it's local. I don't want to drive out of town if I can help it. I'm not good on the roads when it's this slippery, it's lethal. It's Amy, isn't it?'

She nodded. 'It is.' She couldn't remember his name though, so she just smiled.

'What do you say? I'll drop you off at home to make up for driving like an idiot and splashing you.'

Standing still, she realised just how tired she was and nodded. 'That would be appreciated. I mean you don't have to worry about the puddle, I'm just feeling a bit under the weather.'

'Get in, get in. You can direct me to your house, and I'll drop you off, then you can get out of those soaking trousers. My mother was always telling me I'd catch my death through being cold. There is nothing worse.'

Amy smiled at him. 'Thanks, this is very kind of you.'

He shrugged. 'Call it my good deed of the day, to make amends for driving so recklessly.' He rushed to open the door for her, and she got into his car.

'Where to?'

She gave him directions to Cain's house, which was in a tiny little side street. There were six houses and a couple of garages along his street, but it was near to the Co-op which was a life-saver when she needed chocolate or chilli Doritos, her favourite craving at the moment, smothered in mozzarella and covered in sour cream. She realised she was out of crisps and sour cream.

'Actually, if you could drop me off at the Co-op that would be great. I need to grab a few bits and it's near to my house.'

'Of course, that's no problem at all. I can wait for you; I'm in no rush to get back to work.'

'Honestly it's fine, I only live around the corner.'

She closed her eyes, relishing the heat blasting out of the air vents as he drove her home. She never thought that she could drift off in a semi-stranger's car, but she found herself unable to stop herself; the gentle movement of the car was lulling her to sleep.

· · ·

Jerking herself awake, she realised the car was no longer moving, and they were nowhere near to the Co-op.

The car was parked on an unfamiliar lay-by near to a wooded area.

'Where are we?'

'You were having such a lovely little nap I didn't have the heart to wake you. You were so exhausted I thought I'd drive around with you so you could rest, but I'm afraid I'm lost now. I'm not very good with directions, do you have a phone with a satnav?'

Feeling a little disorientated, she pulled her phone out of her pocket and passed it to him. The car engine was running, and he pressed the button to let the window down, then threw her phone out of the window.

'Hey, what are you doing?'

Unclipping her seat belt, she leaned over to release it, and he swung his hand towards the side of her neck that was exposed, hitting it so hard she slumped to the side. Her eyes rolled to the back of her head, and she lost consciousness. And then he smiled.

THIRTY-TWO

Ben, Cain, Scotty and Amber were outside of Anton Highsmith's house. The drive was empty. No orange car in sight and no sightings of it anywhere according to the control room inspector. Cain had on a helmet, knee and elbow pads, gloves and body armour, and he was holding the universal door key otherwise known as a whammer. Ben knocked on the door loudly, and they waited to see if there was any sign of life. Silence greeted them and Ben gave Cain the signal to take out the door, while he and the others stepped backwards to give him enough room to swing the big red metal cylinder.

'It's going to be a mess, boss.' Cain turned to him. 'It's UPVC, you're lucky it's not a composite door or we'd be going in through a window.'

Ben shrugged. 'We have no choice, smash it.'

Cain grinned and with three almighty swings, he smashed the lock, the glass and the plastic to pieces. He finished off by booting the lock hard enough that the door flung open despite hanging off its hinges. Ben thought if anyone was inside the almighty noise of that entrance should have disturbed them from whatever they were doing to come take a look. Cain shouted, 'Police.' Then he was inside, Scotty, Amber and Ben following.

Ben pointed to the stairs, and Scotty and Amber both ran up them, shouting *police*. Cain and Ben began searching the downstairs. Nothing was out of place, nothing was screaming killer at him. In the kitchen there was an adjoining door to the garage. Ben tried the handle thinking it would be locked, but it opened and swung inwards. It was so dark in there, he couldn't see his hand in front of his face. Cain pulled a torch out of his pocket, shining the beam around. There was no car inside of it, but there was an upright fridge freezer and Ben strode towards it, wondering if Aria Burns's face would greet him when he tugged open the door. Sucking in a deep breath he pulled the door open and was greeted by drawers containing frozen pizza, a couple of chicken burgers and some steaks.

'Bollocks.' His voice echoed around the garage.

'What the fuck is going on? What did you do to my front door?'

Both Ben and Cain swung around to see Anton Highsmith's bewildered face staring at them.

Cain lunged for him. 'Get your hands in the air where we can see them.'

Anton did just that, but he was shaking his head. 'What's going on, why have you smashed my door in?'

Ben had a sinking feeling they had the wrong guy, but what had happened this morning, who had he been dragging into his car with force and arguing with?

'Anton Highsmith, you're under arrest for assault and abduction, you do not have to say anything—'

Anton threw back his head and laughed.

This puzzled Ben, and he looked at Cain who shrugged at him. Ben decided to wait until Anton had calmed down before questioning him, and that took a few minutes. Meantime, Scotty and Amber had searched the upstairs and joined them.

'Upstairs is clear, boss, nothing out of the ordinary,' said Scotty.

Anton cleared his throat. 'Just what were you expecting to find up there?'

'We'll talk down at the station.'

'Good and whilst we're waiting for my lawyer, you can get a joiner out to replace my door because I haven't done anything wrong.'

Cain dragged him out of the house towards the van Amber had driven there, making Anton empty his pockets before getting in; there was only a phone and his car keys. He took them off him, then he pulled open the doors and helped, sort of pushed Anton inside.

'Mind your head,' he muttered, almost pushing Anton through the other side of the van. He slammed the doors shut and went round to the front door where Ben was standing.

'I think we have the wrong guy.'

Ben nodded. 'Possibly, but who is to say he doesn't have a lock-up somewhere that he keeps the freezers in; and we still don't know what happened this morning or who the woman is he dragged into his car. There are too many unanswered questions right now that can't be disregarded.'

Ben turned to Scotty. 'You're going to have to call out a joiner and wait for them to arrive.'

'Where are the PCSOs? Why can't they wait?'

'If you can find any, and you ask politely, I'm sure they'll oblige. You're on scene guard until they arrive, but aren't they all up at the health centre?'

Ben turned to Amber. 'When we get back to the station can you get him booked in, please. Then I'll get Amy to interview him with me.'

Cain was removing the arm and leg protectors. 'I can interview him with you.'

'I know, but Amy is good at this kind of thing, and I thought it would give her something more than staring at the wall for a bit.'

'Yeah, good idea. I think she's a bit fed up with everything.'

Amber climbed into the van. 'If you need someone to cover whilst Amy goes off on maternity leave, can I be considered, please?'

Cain arched an eyebrow. 'Who's going to babysit Scotty if you're not with him?'

'I don't bloody care, I'm sick of working with him. I want more out of life, you know, than being stuck in a van with him for the rest of my working days.'

Cain nodded. 'I suppose that's how it should be, you wanting to move on from section.'

'You suppose? You left in a heartbeat when you got offered the chance. Nobody else got a look in.'

'Age and experience before beauty, Amber, I've been at this a lot longer than you.'

She stopped talking but pouted her lips, and Ben couldn't help thinking to himself that he'd rather be a detective down than put up with her attitude. He didn't think Amber would be happy no matter what department she worked in, but she was free to apply just like anyone else when the time came.

Thudding from the back of the van jolted all three of them back to the present moment. They were still no nearer to finding who had dumped Martha MacKay's body into the river. Ben looked around and realised that Anton's car was nowhere to be seen.

'What's he done with his car?'

'Sooner you get him interviewed and made to answer some questions, the better. It goes from bad to worse every hour that passes,' whispered Cain.

Ben couldn't argue with him because it was a disaster of the highest proportions.

THIRTY-THREE

The more Morgan thought about Theo's old church where Martha had last been sighted, the more she thought that everything was pointing towards John. She parked Ben's car and did a double take to see Theo in a pair of faded jeans, boots, black shirt and a starched white dog collar. She jumped out of the car.

'Theo.'

He had been about to disappear inside of the church and turned to see her.

'Wow, Morgan, what's with all the visits? I've never seen you so much, is everything okay? Did you need to get something off your chest? If so, you have caught me at the perfect moment.'

She laughed. 'I'm good and it's great, well it would be glorious if we had the person who killed Martha MacKay locked up, but we're getting there. Are you back at work then?'

'Yes, well, I am doing my best. I can't keep feeling sorry for myself. You inspired me to get out of the bottomless pit I was digging myself into and get dressed. Thanks, Morgan.'

'You don't have to thank me, I'm glad to be of some help. Can we talk for a minute? It might be a little awkward to do out here.'

He looked at her. 'Let's go to the vestry, I need to actually step foot inside the church before I change my mind.'

She noticed his eyes staring down at the floor where he'd been found unconscious and bleeding to death, so she pushed her arm through his. 'Yes, lead the way.'

The church was cold inside and empty much to her relief. She heard Theo sigh and looked at him. He was grinning at her. 'I was terrified Mrs Decker might be around, but it looks like we're both safe. Come on, quick, before anyone decides to pop in.'

He took huge strides to the front of the church then crossed to where the vestry was. He walked inside and both of them said, 'Blimey.' It looked as if a mini tornado had gone off inside the room it was so messy. There were books and papers strewn everywhere.

'Has it been burgled?'

Theo laughed. 'No, it's been Gordoned.'

'What's that?'

'Gordon is a great guy, excellent vicar, but the messiest person I ever did work with. His office always looked like this, well maybe not quiet this bad. I didn't think he'd been here long enough to cause this level of carnage, though.'

Morgan laughed. 'Oh, that's a relief. I didn't want to add a burglary onto my list of jobs today. I have quite enough on.'

Theo began to pick up the sheets of papers and stack them in a pile. Morgan made a start with the various hymn books and Bibles. When there was a space on the desk, Theo sat down and pointed to the other chair. 'Thanks, what did you want to chat about?'

'Theo, this is a little awkward but how well do you know John?'

'Well, he's not like a best friend, I wouldn't put him in the same league as you or Ben. He's more of an old acquaintance. Morgan, I am sorry for the way he was with you yesterday; in fact, I was quite surprised by how rude he was towards you, and it made me a little uncomfortable. I can't imagine how he made you feel.'

'Me too, but it's okay I can put up with bullshit like that. How much do you really know about him?'

Theo nodded. 'Well, he lives or used to live with his mother who was very active in volunteering for the soup kitchen. A lovely woman, nothing was too much trouble for her. I think she's still alive but I'm not sure if she's still helping out at the church or if he moved out. I forgot to ask after her which was very rude of me.'

'What's his surname?'

'Morrison.'

'Do you know his date of birth?'

Theo shook his head. 'Why?'

'Just hear me out and I'll explain. What about Aria Burns, did you know her?'

'No, that name doesn't ring any bells, I'm afraid. Who is she?'

'A woman who went missing just over a year after Martha. She was from the same area, and I wondered if maybe she helped out at the church.'

'I'm not so good remembering names without faces. Do you have a picture, Morgan?'

She pulled out the file she had in her bag and passed him a sheet of paper with Aria's missing person's picture on it. Theo screwed up his eyes and stared at her. 'She does look familiar, I've seen this on the news or in the papers. I was all over the news at the time, but I've never made a point of watching the news, it's far too depressing.'

'Can you ever recollect seeing her in church?'

The tone of her voice was almost pleading with him to say yes so that she could have her connection; if he said she'd been to church then that tied her and Martha to the church, and it also tied them to John Morrison too, if he was there when Aria was.

'Morgan, honestly, I can't say, it was a big church. Where did she work? That might help.'

'St Bee's College.'

Theo stared down at Aria's picture again. 'We used to work with St Bee's a lot. Students would come in to tour the church and see about the different kinds of community work that we did. Maybe she did come in and that's why she looks familiar.'

'Is there any way you could find out if she visited? Would there be records?'

'I don't think so, the college might be able to give you that information. We didn't keep records of visits, there were simply too many different groups, schools and colleges.'

'No, I don't suppose you would. I'm just desperate to find a connection between Aria and Martha; if they were killed by the same guy, then it might be a big lead to finding him.'

'And you think that John Morrison could be that guy, that link?'

She nodded.

'I see, I get why you would think that he was weird when he called this morning. In fact, Declan chased him out and I was relieved to see him go. Declan thought he was awful.'

'Did he tell you the name of the guest house he was staying at in Windermere?'

'No, I didn't ask. I'm sorry.'

'Don't be, how were you to know I was going to come up with this after briefly meeting him yesterday? This could all be some wild chase that I'm on, and it might not mean anything. If you hear from him, please don't tell him we were talking about him. If you do find out where he's staying, please let me know so I can go and talk to him.'

'Of course, I can text him to find out for you but, Morgan, I need you to promise me one thing.'

'What's that?'

'Promise me you will not go and speak to him on your own. If you believe he has anything to do with those missing women, I'm begging you not to put yourself in any danger or at risk of getting hurt.'

'I won't, I promise.'

Theo reached out and took hold of her icy fingers, squeezing them tight. 'Good, that's good. I think you need to be careful.'

Morgan stood up. 'Thank you, Theo, I will. Don't forget to phone me if he replies or turns up here again.'

He nodded and she left him sitting behind his messy desk. She was worried he wasn't ready to be back at work, but then realised, she would be doing exactly the same. What she needed to do was to find John Morrison and fast, before any more women went missing never to be seen for years on end, and hopefully when she found him, she would also find Aria too.

THIRTY-FOUR

Amy began to cough. She felt as if she was choking and tried to reach out for a glass, but she couldn't move her arms. The more she coughed, the more she panicked, and she forced her eyes to open, which felt as if they'd been glued shut. She felt groggy and her throat was sore, it was parched, and she felt as if she'd been out drinking sambuca shots all night, yet she knew that she hadn't because she hadn't touched a drop of alcohol since the day she'd done that pregnancy test in the ladies' toilet at work.

Panic set in as she took in her surroundings. She didn't know this place – whose bedroom was she in? She tried to move again and realised that the reason she couldn't was because she was tied to an armchair. She opened her mouth to scream, but nothing came out except a whisper of a scream. Her voice, there was something wrong with her throat. A door opened behind her and the man who'd offered her a lift walked in. He crouched in front of her.

'Hello, you're back in the land of the living then. This situation is most unfortunate.'

She tried to shout at him, but it just succeeded with her

having an almighty coughing fit. He stood up, took something off the chest of drawers behind him and offered a glass to her lips with a straw. 'Sip this.'

She tried to shake her head, but the pain in the side of her neck was intense.

'It's fine, I haven't poisoned it. I wouldn't know how to do something like that. It's just tap water.' He offered it to her again, and she took the straw into her mouth and sipped.

It felt like she was swallowing tiny shards of broken glass, something must have happened to her throat, but she still forced the liquid down to stop the coughing which also hurt. She also needed to pee really bad.

'Toilet.'

The word was so faint he had to strain to hear her, and his eyes flashed dark at her request.

'This is going to be a struggle for you, and I thought about this a lot when I discovered that you are pregnant. What a shock that was. I never in a million years would have guessed the way you were hiding it. Why did you not tell me this information? Why did you have that all covered up so I couldn't see the facts in front of my eyes? You have made this incredibly difficult for me, and now I am in a dilemma of the sorts that you couldn't begin to imagine. I'll tell you the main problem though, you are never going to fit, it just won't work. I don't have the room for you and that...'

He pointed to her rounded stomach, and she felt a rush of love for the unborn baby inside of her that up until now she hadn't experienced. She knew then that whatever he was planning to do with her she had to survive, her baby was her priority, and she would do what it took to get them both out of here.

'You wouldn't believe the shock and disappointment I felt when I realised you were with child.' He shook his head, and he looked as if she'd hurt him with this when it was the other way around. The sick bastard had hurt her and brought her to God knows where, and she really needed to pee; the baby was pressing down so hard on her bladder it was hurting, and she tried again. 'Toilet.'

He left the room and came back moments later with a big plastic orange bucket that he placed on the floor. In his other hand was a huge knife, and her eyes widened.

'I will untie you; you can pee in that and then I will tie you back up, is that understood? No messing or trying to be heroic, because I will slit your throat and watch you bleed to death on the floor in front of me if I have to. Obviously, I'd rather not, the mess would take forever to clean up, but I need you to know that I have no qualms about doing that should the situation arise.'

Amy couldn't take her eyes off the knife. When she tore them away it was to look at the bucket. Then she felt a sharp pain as the baby moved even further down, pressing harder onto her bladder. She was going to have to relieve herself whether she wanted to or not, and she gave a single nod that sent shockwaves of pain through her body.

'Good, I'm glad we understand each other.'

He bent down and began to untie the bindings around her chest and legs, then he untied her arms. 'I'll turn around to give you some privacy.'

She shook her head and pointed to the door.

'My dear, I am not leaving you unattended for any length of time.'

'You can leave the door open, step outside.' Her words were barely audible.

He thought about it and took a few steps towards the doorway and stood just outside of it, turning his back to her. Her eyes darted around the room. There was a bed, side tables, armchair, wardrobe and a chest of drawers. All of them solid oak, too heavy for her to move or throw and there wasn't even a bedside lamp for her to use as a weapon. There was nothing within her reach that she could use on him. As she tugged down her leggings and underwear, the pain too intense, she squatted over the bucket but felt her cheeks burning at the shame. There was nothing she could use except the bucket of hot urine to throw in his face and maybe give her a few moments to get out of here, but she was disorientated and had no idea where she was. She knew she might not get very far; it was better to wait until she had a bit of strength back and felt strong enough to make her escape. At that point, he might trust her even more. She pulled up her leggings and sat back in the chair, which at least was comfortable and not some hard wooden chair. *Be thankful for small mercies, Amy, then when you've had time to come up with a plan you can smash his head in and run.*

'Are you done?'

'Yes.' Her voice croaked.

He turned around and there was a look of surprise to see her sitting back down; he had obviously thought she would try and escape.

'Oh, well done.' He hurried towards her, placing the knife on top of a dresser so he could retie her.

'Let me go,' she croaked.

He shook his head. 'Can't, I'm in a real mess here and it's all your own fault.'

She tried to nod. 'Won't say anything.'

He tied her tight enough that she couldn't wiggle out of the bindings, and Amy felt hot tears pricking the corner of her eyes.

'I need to think what to do with you, so just be quiet and let me get on with it.'

He left her alone, in pain and terrified for her life. She noticed he hadn't picked the knife back up. It was across the room but she wasn't strong enough to move the armchair without it making a noise. It may as well be out in the garden, but now he'd given her a reason to try and escape. He'd left her with a means to defend herself, and he'd chosen the wrong woman if he thought that she wouldn't use it on him. She would stab him in the blink of an eye if it meant that she could get away from here and keep her baby safe.

THIRTY-FIVE

Amber took Anton to the custody suite to get booked in. He complained the entire time whilst he was fingerprinted about his back being sore. He had swabs for DNA taken, mugshots, then was finally taken into an interview room to wait for Ben. Cain and Ben had gone upstairs to an empty office, which Ben found mildly annoying. He had wanted Amy to assist him interviewing Anton. He knew Morgan was out chasing down leads, so he couldn't really wait for her to come back when Cain was already there.

'Where's Amy?'

Cain shrugged. 'Who knows? Probably at a midwife appointment or something.'

Ben couldn't remember her asking about attending one today, not that it mattered but it wasn't like her to not be here. She was like part of the furniture since she'd had to go on light duties and was supposed to be office bound, even though she kept turning up at crime scenes. 'I guess you'll have to do then.'

'Thanks, boss, can I just say how much I appreciate the value you put on me.'

Ben laughed. 'I didn't mean it like that.'

'Really? You didn't just make it obvious that I was the last resort then or was that all in my imagination?'

Ben tapped the side of his head. 'Let's grab a coffee first before we go down.'

'Don't change the subject. I'll have tea for a change with two sugars. Please.'

'What I meant was that I wanted a woman to assist to see if it made Highsmith feel uncomfortable.'

'Yeah, right. Of course you did.'

Ben didn't answer and went to brew up. He came back in with two mugs and a full packet of biscuits, and Cain's eyes lit up.

'Where did you swipe those from?'

'Peace offering and I cannot divulge my source.'

Cain screwed up his eyes. 'Sounds a bit sus to me, next thing you'll have Madds up here accusing me of stealing from the brew cupboard.'

'I didn't steal them; they were donated to me.'

'Same thing?'

'Definitely not, can you not just be grateful and shut up for two minutes.'

Cain nodded, ripped open the packet and gave him the thumbs up. Which made Ben smile; he took four of them to dunk in his coffee.

'This is nice, bit of male bonding over a tea break. Just me and my boss. We don't get to do this very often. We should make it a regular thing.'

'Cain, shush.' Ben lifted a finger to his lips, and Cain grinned at him. They had roughly three minutes of silence before Marc came storming in, his usual shoving the door far too hard so it slammed into the wall, knocking another chunk of plaster off.

'Where's mine?' He pointed to their mugs.

'Nothing to do with me, boss, blame him.' Cain was

pointing to Ben.

'Give me something, anything, what have you got?'

Cain pushed the packet of custard creams towards Marc, who looked confused.

'Not those, I mean as in an update on where we are finding the person who decided to dump a dead body in our river.'

'We have Anton Highsmith in the cells. Cain and I were going down to interview him.'

'He's here? Have you had his car lifted?'

Ben shook his head. 'Slight problem, he came home on foot, no idea where his car is.'

Marc jumped up off the chair he'd only just sat down in. 'For Christ's sake, is anyone looking for it? It could be a treasure trove of forensics and have a dead body in it and you two are drinking tea like a pair of pensioners on an afternoon out.'

He left the room, and Cain whispered, 'He needs to get over this being offended every time we forget to make him a brew. He's going to have a heart attack at this rate.'

Ben spat coffee all down his tie and used his jacket sleeve to blot it off. 'That was a bit harsh, we got the guy. Come on, let's find out what the hell Highsmith was doing this morning and who with before Marc has a coronary.'

———

Anton sat behind the table, looking a bit too relaxed for someone they were accusing of murder and abduction.

Ben introduced them both.

'Can you state your name and date of birth for the record, please.'

'Anton Highsmith, twenty-first of May 1970.'

'You have declined legal representation, is that correct?'

'Yes.'

'You're sure about that? You asked for a lawyer when we arrested you,' asked Cain.

Anton nodded. 'Quite sure, I thought about it and I haven't done anything wrong. I have nothing to hide.'

Ben scribbled on the large notepad he had in front of him, where he'd listed the questions he was going to ask.

'Where were you this morning around six a.m.?'

Anton sighed. 'Did Jessie phone this in?'

'Who is Jessie?'

'My sixteen-year-old daughter who I was supposed to pick up and drive to Lancaster College at 5.30 this morning.'

'Why would she phone us about that?'

'She is stubborn just like her mum. I was late, and she had already gone to the bus stop and told me to do one. She would rather sit on a bus than in a car with me.'

'Then what happened?' Ben knew what he was going to tell them; he knew that they were most certainly wasting their time if they could prove that he had a daughter called Jessie and she confirmed his story.

'She's a little bitch, I mean, I love her to bits, but her attitude is just horrendous. I lost my temper, got out of the car and dragged her into it. I didn't hurt her, I just dragged her by the elbow, but she was shouting and kicking out at me. I was furious though. I had got up early to take her, even though I have a bad back and I'm on the sick, and I hadn't even gone out for a drink with my mate for his birthday last night so I could drive today.'

'Where is Jessie now?'

'No idea, she was going on a college trip somewhere. Her mum will be able to tell you. Did she ring it in?'

Ben shook his head. 'No, a member of the public was driving past and saw you dragging a woman into your car. She was concerned and she rang it in.'

Anton ran his hand through his hair. 'Bloody hell, I guess it must have looked bad. I don't blame her really, but I swear to

God that it was my daughter, and it was just an angry argument that got a bit out of hand. I never hurt her; I wouldn't do that.'

Ben stood up. 'Do you have the phone number for Jessie and her mum? What's her name?'

'Debbie Graham.'

Ben passed him his notebook and Anton wrote two phone numbers down, with *Jessie* and *Debbie* beside the relevant ones.

'Be right back, do you need a drink or anything? Cain can grab you one.'

Ben left before Anton answered him. He went straight to the custody sergeant's desk and passed her the notebook. 'Can you ring those numbers for me?'

Jo was busy typing and didn't even look up, and she passed him a phone. 'Be my guest.'

Ben tried Jessie's number first.

'What?'

'I'm Detective Ben Matthews calling from Rydal Falls police, is this Jessie Highsmith?'

'Yeah.'

Ben was glad the girl was okay, but felt deflated that Highsmith was telling the truth.

'I need to ask you a couple of questions about this morning. Did your dad pick you up?'

'Eventually, he was late, so I walked to the bus stop.'

'Which bus stop?'

'The one outside the health centre.'

'Did you get in the car with him?'

'I wouldn't say I got in the car willingly with him; he dragged me into it.'

Ben nodded. 'Did he hurt you?'

'No, I probably hurt him. I was kicking him. What's this about?'

'Someone phoned up concerned about you, so I'm checking to make sure that you're okay and didn't come to any harm.'

'I'm good. Where's my dad?'

'He's been arrested for attempted abduction.'

The laughter down the phone was so loud he had to hold it away from his ear.

When it finally stopped, he said, 'Do you think that it's funny your dad is in the cells?'

'Yeah, I do. He didn't do anything though, so you can let him go. He didn't hurt me and he's okay actually. I give him a hard time because I'm a teenager, it's what we do, but he's a good dad. Is he in trouble?'

Ben sighed. 'No, it sounds like it's been a misunderstanding.'

'Okay, I've gotta go, my bus is here.'

She hung up, and Ben passed the phone back to Jo. It didn't mean the guy wasn't their guy, though at least they knew the woman from this morning had been an angry teenage girl who had been attacking him and not the other way around.

He walked back in to see both Cain and Anton chatting, sipping at mugs of coffee.

'Good news, your daughter confirmed it was her and said that you didn't hurt her.'

'So, I can go?'

'Not just yet, where's your car?'

'I dropped it off at the garage and walked home.'

'Which garage?'

'Elliots on Rydal Road.'

Cain took out his phone. 'That's my garage, hang on.'

He left the room and went outside to call them. Two minutes later he was back inside and nodded at Ben.

Anton shrugged. 'Look, I don't know what you think I've done, but you clearly have the wrong guy. The worst thing I've ever done in my life was get a speeding ticket on the A590 five years ago. I'm not who you're looking for. I don't have a vendetta against women; in fact, I would love to have a woman to call my girlfriend. I'm not in the habit of abducting them or pushing them into rivers.'

'You're free to go.'

'Like that, how am I getting home?'

'Cain will drop you off. One last question, Anton. Have you ever been to Birmingham?'

He shook his head. 'Never, I've driven past on my way down to see my brother in Stratford but never been there; and the last time I went to see him was after lockdown but we fell out and I haven't been back that way since.'

'Thanks.'

Ben stayed seated and let Cain take Anton out. He was relieved that Anton hadn't killed anyone this morning, but he was frustrated beyond belief that they still were no closer to finding out who killed Martha MacKay. And who had poor Aria.

THIRTY-SIX

By the time Morgan got back to the station Cain was already walking out of the back door towards his car.

'Where are you going?'

'Home, Highsmith was a no go and seeing as how Amy got to leave early, the boss said I could too.'

'See you tomorrow, say hi to Angela for me.'

He nodded and got into his car. Morgan went to find Ben, who was talking to Marc. Ben gave her a warm smile and she realised how much she'd missed him the last couple of hours.

'Anton Highsmith has been released NFA,' he told her.

'No further action, why? I thought he was looking good and what about the woman he abducted this morning?'

Marc stood up. 'I'll let you fill her in, I'm calling it too. See you tomorrow.'

He left the pair of them staring at each other, and Morgan asked, 'Everyone's leaving, what are we doing?'

Ben glanced at the ancient clock on the wall, and she was aware they had worked well past the end of their shift.

'How did you get on?'

'Spoke to Theo. The more I think about it the more I'm convinced that his friend John could be a viable suspect.'

'Did you get any details on him?' Ben's phone began to ring, and he answered it. 'Declan.'

'Ben.'

'Everything okay?'

'Yes, good. It's the pub quiz, are you up for it? Theo has said he feels like going to the pub and I don't want to put him off, as it's the first time since the attack he's wanted to do anything.'

The office was so quiet Morgan could hear Declan's voice without him being on loudspeaker. She began to nod at Ben and mouthed, 'You should go.'

Ben smiled at her. 'Morgan thinks I should go too.'

'Is Morgan coming too? That would be nice.'

Morgan shook her head. 'No, thanks for the offer but I am in no frame of mind to watch you three lose miserably in front of a pub full of people.'

Declan's laughter filled the air through the speaker.

'Ben, see you at seven.'

Morgan looked at the clock – it was almost quarter to. He put his phone away.

'I don't think—'

'Shush, you need a break now and again. You should go and if anything comes up, I'll message you.'

'You're sure?'

'Yes, go.' She began to shoo him out of the office, and he grabbed his coat off the chair he'd thrown it over on the way in.

'What are you going to do?'

'I'm going to make a phone call and then I'm going home for a long soak in the bath and I'm going to read until my heart is content.'

He leaned forward, his lips brushing her cheek. 'I love you, Brookes.'

'I love you too, Matthews.'

He left her alone; she had been alone a lot the last couple of days, which made a refreshing change from him always feeling the need for her to be babysat. She sat down at her desk and pulled out the file Gulfam had sent to her, searching through it for the few witness statements. She read through them until she came to the one from the neighbour reporting hearing a woman's voice calling out for a dog. There was a mobile number written across the top in black pen and she dialled it, not sure if anyone would answer, but it was worth trying.

'Hello, is this Sheila Grant?'

She was surprised when a voice said, *'Yes, this is Sheila, who is this?'*

Morgan introduced herself and prayed the woman would have something useful to tell her.

'I just wondered if you could talk me through what you heard the night Aria Burns went missing?'

'Where did you say you're from?'

'Rydal Falls police.'

'Is that the Lake District?'

'Yes, I work for Cumbria Constabulary.'

'How come you're asking about Aria? Sorry to be rude but it just seems a bit strange, especially after all this time. It's been years since she went missing, bless her.'

Morgan couldn't argue with her and decided to tell her the truth. 'Were you familiar with Martha MacKay, a woman who went missing a year before Aria did?'

'I heard about some sex worker who went missing, but that wasn't big news. It never is when it's someone like that. I should imagine they go missing quite a lot when it gets too much for them. Poor women, it must be a terrible life.'

'I'm afraid we pulled Martha's body out of a river two days ago.'

'Oh, that's bad. I'm sorry to hear that, but what has this to do with Aria?'

'Nothing at the moment, but I think their cases could be connected.'

'Right, I see. Maybe, you never know.'

'So, can you talk me through that night, please. I have your statement in front of me, but I'd like to hear it from you, maybe you remember something more since you gave it, it's been two years now.'

'I had come back from work about quarter to six and my son, who has since moved out, had been smoking cannabis in my front room all afternoon, and it stank. I hate the smell of it, can't abide it. I was furious with him; he was nowhere to be seen, of course; he'd sneaked off to his mate's house to play Xbox with him. Even though it was the middle of December and freezing, I had to throw open all the windows and even had to open the front door a little, which I didn't like doing when I was on my own, but the smell was making me feel sick.'

'Then what happened?'

'Well, nothing really, I hadn't had time to put the television on. I'd been upstairs and got changed quick, then went back down to shut the front door; you just don't know who's hanging around, do you? I was still raging because now all the heat had escaped, and the inside of the house was as cold as the outside. I went into the front room to shut the windows and heard a woman's voice across the road somewhere in the playing fields, calling out for what I assume was a dog.'

'Can I ask why you thought it was a dog and not a child?'

'Well, it was dark for one thing, it was the middle of winter, freezing cold and I don't know many kids these days called.' She paused. *'What was she shouting? It was old-fashioned. Oh Lord, my memory is terrible. I'd forget my head if it was loose.'*

'Did it sound like a dog's name?'

'Bertha, that's it, she was calling out for Bertha. I don't know many kids these days called Bertha, do you?'

'No, I can't say that I do.'

'Well, I assumed it was a dog but then she shouted, "here, girl, come here," and that confirmed that it was. I closed the windows, put the TV on and ate my Pot Noodle. I never gave it another thought until the police came knocking the next day.'

'Did you know Aria?'

'Not really, I knew her to say hello to. We'd take each other's parcels in, that kind of thing.'

'Did it sound like Aria's voice?'

'I couldn't say, I don't think it did because I never thought it was at the time, but I'd only ever heard her talking normally, I never heard her shouting.'

'Did you ever see her with a dog?'

'Never.'

'Oh.'

'Sorry, petal, is it not what you were hoping to hear?'

'I'm just chasing up the finer details. Do you know of anyone who has or had a dog called Bertha in that area?'

'No.'

'Okay, thank you so much for your time.'

'Good luck, I hope you find the bastard that killed Martha and the person who took Aria.'

Morgan paused. 'Do you think she was abducted?'

'Has to have been. She's never been back here, no one has heard from her since that night. I think something awful happened to her but I'm not the expert, it's just my opinion. Goodbye.'

Sheila hung up, and Morgan checked the notes again, there was no mention of the name Bertha anywhere, at least that was something.'

She pulled her coat on; she was ready for that soak in the bath.

———

As she walked across the atrium she heard Brenda's voice call, 'Morgan, are you busy?'

She stopped and her brain told her to say an emphatic 'absolutely', but her heart, which was far too soft at times and had a soft spot for Brenda, made her turn around.

'No, what's up, Brenda?' She knew immediately she was probably going to regret this if it was a front desk job. She had worked front desk when she was being tutored and it had been enlightening to say the least. The people who turned up on a daily basis had never failed to surprise her.

'There's a woman, bit doddery on her feet, thinks she saw a dead body in a car this afternoon.'

Morgan closed her eyes for the briefest of moments, regret kicking in big time.

'Sorry, Morgan. I've shouted over the radio three times now for an available officer and they're all tied up. There's no one around and it's a bit late for her to be out in this weather.'

'Is she a regular customer?'

Brenda shook her head. 'No.'

Pursing her lips and blowing a long breath through them, she went to one of the side rooms and opened the door into the waiting area. There was a teenage boy with a man whom Morgan assumed was his dad, and a woman on her own. Morgan smiled at her.

'Do you want to come through?'

The woman stood up, leaning heavily on a walking stick, and followed her into the small room. Morgan pointed to a chair and sat in the one on the opposite side of the small table.

'How can I help you?'

'I don't know if you can really, but I thought I better tell someone, or I wouldn't sleep tonight.'

'I'm Morgan and you are?'

'Elizabeth Short.'

'What did you see, Elizabeth?'

'I was coming home from the knit and natter club around three this afternoon, and I saw this dirty old brown car driving past me. I couldn't help but notice the woman in the passenger seat was slumped against the glass. The side of her face was a bit slack, and she looked.' Elizabeth paused. 'Well, she looked dead.'

Morgan didn't know if she had the capacity for this after the day she'd had.

'What made you think she was dead?'

'If she wasn't dead, she was unconscious. I worked as a nurse up until I retired, and I know a dead body when I see one.'

'Can I ask why you are just reporting it now?'

'I talked myself out of it, told myself I was being ridiculous that nobody would be driving around here with a dead woman in the front of the car. Then I read yesterday's newspaper which I never read yesterday and saw that they'd pulled a woman out of the river, and I'm worried in case this man has killed another one and was taking her to throw her into the river as well.'

There was a pile of scrap paper on the table. Morgan uncapped a pen and began to write on it.

'What make or model of car was it?'

'I don't know cars, but it was quite old. I'd say a good ten years.'

'Did you get the registration number?'

'No, sorry.'

'What about a description of the driver?'

'I wasn't looking at him, I couldn't take my eyes away from her, the dead woman.'

'What did she look like?'

'Dark blonde, a bit of a reddish tint to it.'

Aria had light blonde hair in her missing photo. Could it have been her? she wondered. 'Anything else?'

Elizabeth shook her head. 'I'm not very good, am I?'

Morgan smiled at her. 'It's difficult to remember, don't worry. What direction did it drive?'

'Well, it was driving away from here so maybe Bowness, Windermere. What will happen now, will you go and search for it?'

'I will let the duty sergeant know and he will get officers to keep an eye out for it. Is there any chance the woman could have been in a deep sleep?'

Elizabeth paused and a look of doubt crossed her face. 'Well, I suppose she might have been.'

It took all of Morgan's self-control not to sigh out loud, but she didn't and managed to keep it inside. 'Thank you, Elizabeth, we will make some enquiries and if we need to speak to you again someone will be in touch; we have your details now. I'll give them to Sergeant Madden to keep hold of. It's his shift on nights tonight, and they'll do a search for the car.' She stood up and opened the door for the woman, who smiled at her.

'Thank you, goodnight, I hope you find her and she's okay.'

Then she hobbled off out of the front doors, and Morgan waved at Brenda who was behind the desk. It was time to go home but not before passing Elizabeth's intel onto Madds.

THIRTY-SEVEN

Ben refused to tell Morgan the position the team came in at the quiz last night over breakfast, which meant they came last. 'I don't know why you can't just say it out loud, there's no shame in being the biggest losers in the pub.'

Ben shook his head. 'The cheek of it.'

'You know, for three men who are highly intelligent your general knowledge is abysmal.'

'I'm not going to disagree with you on that one.'

'How was Theo?'

'He seemed a lot brighter, more like his old self. Oh, he gave me an address for you for his creepy mate John; he said you were after it.'

'He did, that's good. I think we seriously need to look into John Morrison, he is ringing all the alarm bells.'

'We have nothing to lose, so let's get to work and see what we need to do.'

Cain was in the office but no Amy; he nodded at them both as they walked in.

'Morning.'

Morgan smiled at him. 'Morning, Cain, did you chat to Angela about Amy's predicament?'

'I did better than that; actually she was the one who brought it up first, but she asked me to move in with her, said she'd move in with me in a heartbeat but she loves her pink kitchen slightly more than she loves me, so I'd have to live with her.'

'What did you say?'

'Well, yes, what else is there to say? I mean the pink kitchen isn't the manliest of kitchens to cook in, but then again, I think baby pink suits my colouring.'

Morgan giggled. 'Have you told Amy?'

He shook his head. 'She's not here yet.'

'Oh, maybe she slept in. I'll ring her and see if she needs picking up. It will cheer her up no end not having to worry about moving out of yours. Are you going to draw up a formal contract?'

'Angela said she'd sort it out with her solicitor. As soon as Amy turns up, I'll tell her.'

'I've said it before and I'll say it again, you are a big softie deep down, Cain, and one of the nicest people I know.'

Ben walked out of his office. 'Steady on, his head is big enough without you making it swell even more. Where's Amy?'

Morgan and Cain both shrugged, and Morgan phoned her, but it went to voicemail.

'She'll be here soon, unless she's phoned in sick. She said she felt unwell yesterday and had a headache.'

'Well, nobody has bothered to pass the message on to me if she did, but that's no great surprise.' He clapped his hands together so loud the noise echoed around the room, making Morgan jump.

'Let's get something moving today. Highsmith was a letdown. Morgan, let's focus on this John, what was his name?'

'John Morrison.'

'Yeah, him. We have no other leads, and he set Morgan's

bad guy internal radar off big time. Let's do a deep dive into his background and see if he's got previous for anything. Once we know about that we'll go pay him a visit, see if he's got any extra-large freezers in his home.'

'Just a slight problem with that, boss?'

He looked at her. 'What's the problem?'

'He's staying here on holiday; I don't think he'd bother to bring his freezers with him unless he's super strong and has a truck to move them around in.'

'Brookes, did you have to burst my bubble like that? We can at least go speak to him, it's better than nothing. What if he has family in the area? I mean he could have been blatantly lying about where he's stopping. If there is anything in his intel, can you do an address search to see if anyone with his surname lives around here, and we'll get West Midlands police to go search his home. Is that better for you?'

She smiled at his sarcasm. 'Yes, boss.'

'Good. Go grab me a coffee, please. I have a headache.'

She left him to go and make the drinks. After placing the mug on Ben's desk Morgan began to search through the system for any other Morrisons living in the area, but couldn't find any. She clenched her knuckles and stuffed one hand in her mouth to stop herself from screaming out loud. It would have been so good to get a more permanent address for him. Squeezing her eyes tight shut, she counted to five; at least they had something to work on. She couldn't wait to see John take his turn at squirming once she and Ben began to question him. He was one guy she was really going to enjoy making cringe.

THIRTY-EIGHT

Marc agreed that Morgan should go with Cain to talk to John Morrison, so they left as soon as she'd told Ben there were no obvious relations living in the area, and after she had scrutinised his intelligence report. Which had been equally as disappointing: there was nothing much to go on, a couple of incident logs from him reporting hassle from a neighbour, but that was years ago. For such a creep he had a clean record, which Morgan had found to be more than a little bit disturbing. He reminded her of those serial killers that were big into religion and church. It always came back to BTK for Morgan out of all the weirdos who killed. She found him the worst and the one who had given her nightmares after she had read a true crime book about him and watched some documentaries. The fact that he could murder an entire family in cold blood and sexually assault a child before killing her, then go home to his own wife and kid, made her blood run cold. Did he picture his wife as one of his victims when he was sleeping with her? She shuddered and Cain glanced at her. 'Are you coming down with something, that's twice you've done a full body shiver.'

'No, I just keep thinking about serial killers.'

'Morgan, you're not right in the head; you know that, don't you? It's not normal to think about that stuff all the time, it might turn you into one. Does Ben know about this sick fetish you have? Is he not terrified you'll stab him to death in the night? Because I'm telling you, you're scaring me and I don't have to live with you.'

She looked at him. 'Shut up, Cain, it's not like that. I've told you before, they fascinate me. I'd love to have done a criminal psychology degree and worked in Broadmoor.'

'What? So you could chat to Peter Sutcliffe and Ian Brady?'

'Sutcliffe is dead, thank God, and so is Brady, who was at Ashworth Hospital in Liverpool.'

'See. How do you even know this stuff off the top of your head, Morgan? Although it's handy you do, because is that what makes you so ace at catching killers?'

'It's research, Cain. What do you do on your days off?'

'Eat food, hang around with Angela, watch Netflix, drink wine. Like most normal people.'

'Are you still running?'

'From what?'

'You know what I mean, to keep fit.'

He shook his head, then patted his stomach. 'It's no fun when I haven't got anyone to be in competition with since you wimped out. Angela is a bad influence on me, she keeps plying me with food and drink, be rude to say no.'

He stopped the car behind the knackered old Volvo across the street from the Windermere Lodge B&B. 'That's his car, look at the size of his boot, it's the perfect space for transporting a dead body in. Can I check his tyres now, find something worth bringing him in for?'

He winked at her, and she grinned. 'You're right, it is big enough to get a body into though.'

'Oh, yes. It's big enough to get a Sasquatch into the back of that.'

'Bet his freezer couldn't fit Bigfoot in it though.'

They walked into the guest house, and a guy who was hoovering the hallway stopped to look at them. He switched the hoover off. 'Do you have reservations? We don't allow guests to check in until three p.m.'

Morgan tugged out her warrant card and held it up. 'We're looking for John Morrison, is he here?'

The guy nodded and pointed to a room at the end of the corridor. 'Room one.' He switched the hoover on again and continued.

Cain led the way. He knocked a little too loudly on the door, and a voice called out, 'I don't need any towels today.'

Cain arched an eyebrow at Morgan. 'Were we offering?' He hammered even louder, and the door was thrown open. Morrison stood there staring at Morgan with a look of surprise on his face.

'What do you want?' Then he looked up at Cain, who towered above him by a good head and shoulders.

'I want to chat to you, John. Can we come inside?'

Before he could answer, Cain was stepping inside the room and John had no choice but to retreat or be crushed by Cain who wasn't stopping for anyone. John stumbled backwards, almost landing on his bed.

'What's this about?'

'I'm not sure if you remember what Theo told you I do for a living, but I'm a police detective and right now I'm on enquiries for a murder investigation. Your name has unfortunately cropped up on those enquiries, so I'd like to have a little chat with you. Would you like to do that here or would you prefer to come to the station.' She smiled at him and didn't miss the look of fear in his eyes.

'I don't know what you're talking about, what murder investigation?'

'Martha MacKay.'

'What? What has that got to do with me?'

'That's what I'm here to find out, John.'

Morgan's phone began to vibrate in her pocket, but she ignored it. It stopped and started again. 'Excuse me.' She stepped outside of the room to see Ettie's name on her screen.

'Ettie, are you okay?'

'*No, Morgan. Dear God, there's another body, another woman.*'

Morgan looked at Cain. 'Cuff him, we need to get him to the station.'

John held up his hands. 'Are you insane? For what reason, I'm here on holiday.'

But Morgan was talking to Ettie. 'Where are you?'

'*Same place, I couldn't stop thinking about her, Martha I mean, and I thought I'd go take some flowers to put on the riverbank near to where she was, and I saw her.*'

Ettie let out a sob.

'*She's only partly in the water. It's high after the snow began melting and...*' There was a slight pause. '*Her head is bent at a funny angle. Morgan, I think that her neck is broken.*'

'Ettie, I'm on my way. Have you called it in?'

'*Not yet, I wanted to tell you.*'

'I need you to ring 999 and tell them, please, so patrols can get travelling. I'm not in a marked vehicle. Can you do that for me?'

'*Yes, I can.*'

Morgan ended the call. Cain had John cuffed and had read him his rights and was walking out to the car. He asked, 'What's going on?'

'Body.'

Cain let out a groan. John, who was complaining loudly, stopped when he heard the word body. The colour draining from his face, he looked at Morgan.

'This is nothing to do with me.'

She glared at him. As Ettie's call came over the radio, she phoned Ben.

'Ettie has found another body by the river.'

'Fuck.'

'We have Morrison cuffed and in the back of the car, but I need to get to the scene.'

'I'll wait for you, tell Cain to put his foot down.'

Cain raced back to the station where Ben's car was idling, waiting for her to jump in. Ben leaned out of the window.

'Cain, get him booked in for interview, and can you try and find Amy? When you get hold of her, I need you down at the scene as soon as he's in a cell and she can interview Morrison.'

Cain gave him a salute as Ben sped away towards Covel Woods once more.

THIRTY-NINE

He was feeling pleased with himself after spending hours trying to figure out what to do. He'd realised he had no choice but to make more room in the freezer. It wasn't as if he could release her now. She was a cop, not only that she was a pregnant cop which made it a hundred times worse. This had been the worst mistake of his life, and he should never have stopped to offer her a lift. It had been the voice inside his head that had told him he could do it, that blackness inside of him that was threatening to devour his soul.

The fight was all too real for him of good versus evil. He wanted to be a nice guy, a good guy, but the battle raging inside of his head was ferocious and, unfortunately for Amy, it had won and now here they were in the most problematic situation of his life. It was only a matter of time before he gathered himself together enough to do what he had to do. He had taken care of a few things he should have taken care of earlier and was feeling quite satisfied with himself. It had been risky taking her there, but it was the only place he could think where he could dump her and hopefully wash away any of that pesky DNA all the crime shows kept telling him would get him caught.

The house was wonderfully silent without his mother here. He could get used to this life of freedom, being able to eat what he wanted, go wherever he fancied and watch the television until his brain turned to mush. All those things he was limited to do when she was strutting around the house with that permanent scowl of displeasure at her entire life. She wore that look of contempt like a badge of honour, and he realised it had been far too long living under her shadow of unhappiness. He began to scrub at the kitchen worktops all the same, with the bleach he insisted she use once a week to kill all the bacteria and germs that thrived on it. As he scrubbed with the smiley faced scrubber, he smiled back at it. The peace was lovely until he heard a loud thump come from upstairs. He paused; sometimes next door's kids were banging around all hours of the day. He rarely noticed the shouting, screaming, swearing and pounding of footsteps up and down their stairs anymore, but this sounded like it had come from the spare room where he was keeping his guest. It didn't happen again so he carried on scrubbing. He had moved the armchair into the middle of the room so she couldn't reach the walls to kick or pound her fists against them for help. There was nothing within her reach. She couldn't do anything except bang on the floor, which was the reason he would have to do something about her sooner rather than later.

As soon as he'd finished cleaning, he'd go check on her; maybe she needed to pee. He hadn't realised quite how often pregnant women needed to do that and he disliked having to swill out the bucket every four hours. Leaning over he switched the radio on and turned the volume up, just in case she decided to start thumping on a regular basis. If next door asked what he was doing he would tell them a bit of DIY, finally getting around to sorting out the nails in the floor in the spare room, and if it carried on too long then he'd use the hammer to smash her head in, that would silence her.

FORTY

There was a police van abandoned in the middle of the car park. Ben parked alongside it and Morgan jumped out. Not hesitating to put protective clothing on, she ran to see Ettie standing on the path that led towards the river. Hugging her aunt fiercely, she whispered, 'Are you okay?'

'I am, but this is terrible, Morgan. It's so sad and I'm a little bit scared that someone is trailing dead women through my beautiful woods. These poor girls.'

'Me too, Ettie, can you go home and make yourself a hot drink? I'll be with you as soon as I've assessed the scene.'

Ettie nodded. 'Those two police officers from the other day are already there.'

'Thank you.'

Morgan knew she should go back to get suited and booted, but the likelihood of the killer carrying the body from his car to the river was very slim, unless he was super strong and extremely foolish because it was a popular area for families and walkers. It was more feasible that he dumped the body where Wendy took the tyre casts from. People walked here and parked in this car park at all hours of the day, it was especially popular with some of the local teenagers who liked to park up at night and just chill. When she'd been a patrol officer back in the day of being in company with Dan, he'd brought her here and told her that as long as they weren't being a nuisance, doing drugs or leaving a mess he left them to it. She'd once asked Ettie if they bothered her and she'd shrugged and said if I can't hear them, then they're no bother.

The chances were he had put the body into the river at the same place as Martha, which meant they'd missed him. They should have been guarding it but who was to know he would do it again so soon? A voice inside her mind whispered, *you knew though, didn't you? That uneasy feeling you've been carrying around since Martha was found was this. You knew it would happen again, and you still don't know for sure who he is.* That niggling voice was right. She didn't know if it was John. Oh, how she hoped in her heart that it was, but what if she was wrong about him? Yes, he was a total creep, but it didn't mean he was their man. If he was, he had managed to do this right under her nose, and she wasn't going to forgive herself for that.

She saw the two officers standing on the riverbank, next to Ben, a body on the ground next to them, and she wondered if this was how she would meet Aria Burns. As Morgan rushed forwards, she stopped and stared at the body. The woman was much older than Aria's picture. She was fully clothed, her head bent at a strange angle.

'Where was she?'

One of the officers turned to Morgan. 'Caught up in the bushes. I don't think she's been in the water very long.'

'Do you know her, Morgan?' Ben asked, and she shook her head, unable to tear her gaze away from the body. 'I don't think so.'

'She doesn't look like Martha's body did. There must only be hours in her being dumped and Ettie finding her. Oh God.' She cupped a hand to her mouth.

'What's wrong?'

The horror Morgan felt was threatening to take over and she had to suck in a deep breath. 'As I was leaving work last night, a woman came in to report a car that drove past her with a woman slumped in the front passenger seat who looked dead or unconscious.'

Ben's eyes widened. 'When did she see it?'

'Around three p.m. yesterday afternoon. It was gone eight o'clock when I spoke to her at the front desk. She said a dirty brown car, no reg, no model, or make, no description of the woman apart from blonde, red hair, didn't see the driver and said it headed in the direction of Bowness or Windermere.'

'What did you do?'

'I passed it onto Madds for his shift for observations; there wasn't much to go on. She was quite elderly, and the information was so vague I assumed it might be someone who'd fallen asleep.'

'Someone needs to talk to her. Get Amy to do it.'

Morgan took out her phone to ring Amy, but it still went straight to voicemail, once maybe, but twice was highly unlikely. She turned to see Cain strolling towards her. 'I can't get hold of Amy. Do you think she's okay?'

Cain looked worried. 'I don't know, I haven't seen her since yesterday. I couldn't find her at the station so came to see if she had already come here to the scene. When did you last speak to her?'

'When she left yesterday afternoon to walk home.'

'What time was that?'

'About quarter to three.'

The churning in her stomach made her feel queasy, and she turned to Ben. 'I know this is important, but neither me nor Cain have spoken to Amy since yesterday, she's not turned in and not answering her phone. Can we go check she's okay and not ill or something?'

'Morgan, you go, I can't spare the both of you right now.'

Cain gave her the keys to the car, and as he leaned forward, he whispered, 'I have a bad feeling about this, ring me as soon as you find her.'

Pulling his own set of car keys from his pocket, he said, 'There's a front door key on there.'

Morgan nodded and left them standing there waiting for Declan to arrive.

Amy was probably asleep or at a midwife appointment; the chances of anything happening to her were ridiculously slim. She didn't seem to be a magnet for angry, sick killers like Morgan was.

———

Morgan parked behind Amy's car and dashed to the front door. She knocked and waited all of five seconds before opening the door and going inside.

'Amy.'

Her voice was loud enough to echo back to her, but the house was silent, and she knew that she wasn't here, but she checked each room to be sure, scared in case she found her collapsed somewhere or in bed poorly.

When she came back down, she sat on the bottom stair and phoned Cain.

'She's not here, no sign of her. No dirty pots in the sink. It doesn't even smell of her perfume; she wears Chanel Mademoiselle, and it lingers in the air, so I don't think she slept here, her bed is made.'

'She always makes her bed, but she doesn't always put the breakfast pots away. What about her coat and handbag, are they hanging over the banister or in the cupboard under the stairs?'

They weren't hooked over the stair post next to her and she

stood up to check in the cupboard. 'The coat she was wearing yesterday isn't, but her car's outside.'

'Maybe she walked to work and we're all panicking because she hasn't answered her phone. It could have died on the way in.'

'Yeah, maybe.' But Morgan wasn't convinced. 'I'll go check the office see if she's there.'

She hung up and let herself out of Cain's house. As she was locking it the woman from next door walked up her path.

'Hi, have you seen Amy today?'

'No, I saw her yesterday on her way out but not today.'

'Okay, thanks.'

She smiled at the woman, but it didn't cover the tight knot of nerves that were forming inside of her stomach. This wasn't like Amy, she didn't do drama, she wouldn't ignore her calls; in fact, she hated a fuss and would be mildly annoyed that Morgan was so worried about her, but she was her friend and she couldn't stop the feeling that something awful had happened to her.

FORTY-ONE

Declan stared at the elderly woman on the ground. 'She looks familiar.'

'She does?' Ben's voice a little higher at this revelation.

Declan was the only one out of them sufficiently suited and booted to go near her, and he stepped forwards and tilted his head. 'Looks like a broken neck. I should imagine there will be sufficient bruising when I get her in the mortuary for examination.' He crouched down next to her, and taking her head in both hands he whispered, 'I'm sorry, I just need to look at something.' Gently lifting her head, he rolled it the other way slightly to see a large purple bruise on her neck and nodded. 'Yep, thought so.' Placing her head back down he stepped back.

'I'm going to go out on a limb here and it's not something that I would do lightly. You know how much I prefer cold, hard evidence rather than second guessing, but I think I can say with as much conviction as I can muster that whoever killed Martha, killed her. It's the same method of death, the bruising around the neck in a similar position to Martha's. Look I'm sure I recognise her, maybe from Theo's church. Is it okay to send him a pic of her face and ask her if he does? Have you got an ID for her yet?'

'Not yet and be my guest. You better warn Theo she's dead before you send it though. He might not have the stomach for this like we do.'

Declan smiled. 'I will, I'm not that mean.' He leaned in close and took a quick snap of the victim's face.

Theo, I'm at a crime scene and I think we might know the victim, well I think you will know her more than I do. She looks familiar. Are you okay with me sending a pic of her?

Three dots appeared on Declan's phone.

Yes, is she okay?

Not really, she's dead. Will you be okay if I send it? Don't say yes if you're not.

An extra-large thumb appeared on the screen, so Declan sent it, and Ben waited, almost holding his breath. If they could ID her already, it would make all the enquiries so much easier and save a lot of time.

This is awful. Are you for real or is this some sick joke?

Declan showed Ben the message. 'Mary mother of Jesus, maybe he wasn't ready for it after all.'

Ben stifled his laughter, it wasn't funny in the least, but Declan was such a natural comedian, it just came out of nowhere and he didn't even try. They waited and waited until eventually the three dots that seemed to be teasing them disappeared.

That is Mrs Decker.

Declan muttered. 'Oh dear.' He turned around to look at the woman again, closer, and realised that was exactly who she was.

'Who is Mrs Decker?' asked Ben.

Declan pointed to the body. 'She is.'

'How do you both know her?'

Declan walked away from the body and lowered his voice. 'I don't like to talk bad about the dead, you know that. But she is one of the women from the church who drives Theo a little bit crazy. She's very outspoken and apparently, she's been trying to arrange a semi-naked photoshoot with the other women to raise funds by standing there with nothing but a pair of Chelsea buns covering their breasts. Theo had been most worried about it. I guess he doesn't need to be now.'

Ben's head was pounding, he'd had too many drinks at the pub quiz last night and woken up with a slight hangover, and this confusion wasn't helping it to improve.

'Help me out here, please. Why would Mrs Decker—' He stopped and looked at her. 'Dear God, is she a sex worker in her spare time? That would connect her to Martha.'

Even Declan looked horrified. 'I don't think so, Ben, she's a respected member of the church.'

'Then why is she dead? Killed the same way as Martha MacKay and her body in the same deposition site?'

'Way beyond me, my friend, I'm just the doc who dices and slices to tell you how they died, not why.'

Ben thought this day could not get any worse and then his phone rang. He saw Morgan's sweet face smiling up at him.

'Did you find Amy, is she okay?'

Morgan's voice was high-pitched, a hint of hysteria in it.

'No, I can't find Amy anywhere. I've checked the house, the

station, I've looked through her drawers for any hospital letters, her phone's dead and I don't know what to do.'

'Christ.' Ben scrubbed his hand across his face. 'Where the hell is she then?'

'You better start ringing around the hospitals in case she's been in an accident. Ben, that woman who came in to report a woman slumped against the car window last night. Amy has blondish, red hair, and she left the station at quarter to three. It was approximately three when whoever it was drove past in that car. What if it was her? What if someone hurt her and took her?'

Ben felt the forest around him begin to spin, the trees were blurring, and he began to get tunnel vision. He stumbled backwards against the trunk of a thick Scots pine tree, could feel the rough bark pressing into the back of his neck.

'Ben, are you okay? What's wrong?'

Morgan's voice sounded a million miles away, and he closed his eyes, his phone falling to the ground, when he felt an almighty slap against the side of his cheek, it was stinging hard.

His eyes flew open to see Cain standing in front of him.

'Sorry, boss, but you looked like you were going to pass out. Thought I'd snap you out of it.' Cain didn't look in the least bit remorseful.

Declan was standing watching the pair of them with a look of amusement on his face. 'Ben, are you okay, do you need medical assistance?' he asked.

Morgan's voice came through the speaker on his phone that was on the floor.

'Will someone tell me what the fuck is happening and what I'm supposed to do about Amy?'

Cain picked up the phone. 'What about Amy? And he's okay, he went a bit dizzy that's all. He's fine.'

She told Cain what she'd told Ben, and he turned to look at Ben.

'Sorry, you're going to have to call in backup from Barrow or

Penrith to deal with this. Are you hearing what Morgan's saying? Amy is missing. We have to go find her now.'

'Go, you go. I'll see what I can do.'

Wendy, who had arrived along with Joe just in time to see Cain slap Ben, was standing there, jaw slack and mouth open in awe.

'What the hell is going on here? Why are you all over my crime scene and not even suited up. Get out of here, all of you!'

The two coppers who had been standing next to the body, Declan and Ben all stepped back.

Declan's arm threading through Ben's, he whispered, 'I'll take you back to the car.'

Ben didn't shrug him away. His feet felt as if they didn't belong to him and he let Declan guide him to his car.

Helping him into the passenger seat he passed him a can of fizzy Vimto.

'You need some sugar and you'll be fine.'

Ben took a huge glug then he rested his head against the cool leather and tried to get his brain to function again.

FORTY-TWO

Morgan went downstairs to find the duty sergeant and was relieved to see Daisy in the office where Madds usually was.

'Hey, Daisy, are you not on Task Force now?'

'Not for the moment, I'm doing my acting sergeant and got put on this shift.'

'Good, we have a huge problem. Amy is missing.'

Daisy leaned forward. 'Our Amy from your office, where is she?'

'I don't know, she left yesterday, and nobody has seen or heard from her since. She didn't turn up for work. It's not like her. I've never known her not come in. Her house is empty and there is no sign she's been home. I'm scared for her safety; we have some lunatic dumping women's bodies in the river, and they keep washing up in Covel Woods...'

Morgan didn't finish her sentence; she didn't want to say what she was thinking out loud in case she made it come true.

'We need to get a log on about it, then arrange teams to go searching for her.' Daisy paused. 'I think.'

Morgan nodded. 'Yes, we do. We need patrols out visiting

anywhere she could be, her parents, Jack's house – is he on shift today?'

'Yes, he is. I'll call him back here. He might know something, although it's unlikely after the almighty bust-up they had a while back.'

Daisy called Jack on the radio whilst Morgan phoned the control room and asked them to log everything. Cain went sprinting past the office to the stairs, and Morgan stood up.

'In here, Cain.'

He turned, saw her and came rushing into the office.

'What's happening? Daisy, what are you doing here?'

'Acting sergeant,' Daisy and Morgan said at the same time.

'First shift?'

She nodded.

'Bloody hell, did you know about the body at Covel Woods too?'

'A high risk misper and a dead body in my first hour. You have to be kidding me?'

'Sorry, I'm sad for the dead woman, but our priority right now is locating Amy. Morgan, let's go; we can start visiting anyone who knows Amy. Daisy, circulate Amy's picture to your shift and tell them to be on the lookout for her, please.'

'Yes, will do.'

Morgan smiled at Daisy. She looked like Morgan did her first day out on independent patrol before that shift went horribly wrong. She'd been excited at the prospect of being her own boss, yet terrified at the same time. 'You got this, Daisy. Get the misper log updated, home address searched, neighbour spoken to by myself. With no sign of Amy, the neighbour had nothing to report. Ben will handle the body by the river, that's not something you need to worry about except for staff to scene guard until she's been taken away by the undertakers.'

Daisy gave Morgan a half smile. 'Thank you, I know this,

it's just hard to remember when you're the one supposed to be in charge.'

'Get the PCSOs rounded up for scene guard, but don't leave them out there for hours freezing to death, make sure you rotate them. My aunt will sort hot drinks out for them, I'm sure of it.'

Cain took hold of Morgan's arm and dragged her out of the office. 'See you later, Daisy.' Then he was dragging her towards the lift as Marc came running down the stairs in full body armour. Cain let out a groan. 'Who let Robocop out of his office?'

Marc made eye contact with Cain and came running towards him. 'What's the plan, where are we searching?'

Cain closed his eyes and tried to remember who Amy's friends were. 'She didn't leave the house much; she worked and came home to either rage clean or cry about her situation. Her parents live in Kendal so someone should definitely go speak to them.'

Marc nodded. 'Let a Kendal patrol deal with them.'

Cain stared at him. 'Boss, she's one of us not some random person off the street. They deserve to be visited by you or Ben at least, you're her supervisor.'

Marc looked as if he was going to swear but stopped himself. 'Address, I'll go there now. What are you both doing?'

Ben came into the station, his face a little paler than it had been when she'd left him. He came to join them.

'What's happening?'

'The boss is going to speak to Amy's parents in case she's there.'

'Are we panicking a little, being a bit premature, do you think? Has anyone checked the duty sheet to see if she didn't put some last-minute leave in?'

Nobody answered, so Ben did. 'I'll do that. Boss, you go see her parents. Morgan, Cain where do you want to be?'

Cain shrugged. 'I don't know what to do.'

'Go back and check the house. Has anyone spoken to Jack just in case they've kissed and made up?'

Morgan pointed to the office where Daisy was on the phone. 'Daisy is speaking to him now.'

'Good, what's Daisy doing in there?'

'Acting sergeant.'

'Oh, crap, what a day to start that.'

Everyone nodded. 'Should we go up to the office and see what we need to do, instead of standing here getting in everyone's way?'

Morgan called the lift and when the doors opened all three of them got inside whilst Marc waved them goodbye and went to speak to Amy's parents.

―――――

Once they were back in the office Cain went and sat at Amy's desk, and he began rummaging through her drawers. Ben glanced at Morgan who wanted to tell Cain that Amy would probably deck him if she came in and caught him.

'She left at quarter to three, and that woman saw a car with an unconscious woman or who she thought was an unconscious woman, in the front seat around three. Is she reliable, have you checked her out to see if she's like a persistent caller or of sound mind? We could be panicking for no reason. What if the unconscious woman was Mrs Decker? By the way, do we even have a first name for her?'

Morgan shrugged. 'I assumed that the woman she was reporting was just asleep.' Her phone began to ring.

'Hey, Theo, are you okay?'

'I'm not, I feel terrible. I have had the worst bad thoughts about Mrs Decker the past couple of months and now this. Is she

really dead? You know, sometimes Declan has a wicked sense of humour, but that photo.'

The line went silent, and she felt bad; it made her feel terribly sad that she had got so used to dealing with dead bodies that she didn't blink when faced with one, at least not until she would lie awake in the early hours of the morning, unable to sleep for thinking about them, but that was a different story.

'I'm sorry, it's hard to see people like that. Do you know where she lives, if she has any family?'

'I literally know nothing about her except that she terrified me on some deeper level with her ideas and brassiness. I can find out about her though. I can ask the other ladies when they turn up this afternoon.'

'Yes, please. That would be great, thank you so much. Can you message me as soon as you've spoken to them?'

'What do I do, should I mention she's dead?'

'No, we need to notify her next of kin first, Theo.'

'Yes, yes, of course you do. Gordon will be upset; he had kind of gotten used to her. I'm not going to enjoy telling him; of course, when you say the time is right, then I will. Her poor family are going to be devastated.'

'Maybe go home and drink a cup of sugary tea and wait until we have an update for you before you speak to anyone, even Gordon. Is that okay with you?'

'Of course.'

She ended the call, then logged in to her computer. She needed to see how many Mrs Deckers there were in the area. Somehow, she didn't think there would be many as it wasn't a common name; at least she didn't think it was. Picking up her radio she called the control room and asked them to do a voter's check for the name Decker. When they replied, she was surprised to see there were two Deckers, one in Rydal Falls, the other in Ambleside. She would have bet any amount of money on them being related. Morgan scribbled down their addresses: this was a tough call. Someone needed to go and inform the family about Mrs Decker, but she wanted to search for Amy too. Cain was standing up and heading out of the door.

'I'm going to my house to do another look around, then I'll have a drive around, if that's okay with you, boss?'

Ben nodded. 'Morgan, I need to find out Mrs Decker's address. Are you okay to come with me and go knock and see if she lives in either of those houses?'

She nodded. 'Should we go now?'

His phone began to ring, and she heard Wendy's voice as he put her on loudspeaker.

'I need you back at the scene, Ben. I can't release it. The undertakers are insisting the DS authorises and signs the paperwork.'

'Tell them I said it's okay.'

'I did and they said they have to speak to whoever is in charge. I don't know where they found these two muppets, but they haven't got a brain between them. The sky's gone really dark, and the weather's going to turn, it's going to pour down. We could do with getting her body out of the elements, so we don't lose precious forensics.'

Ben slammed the palm of his hand down on the desk, and Wendy whispered, *'Believe me, I want to slam my fist into the jobsworth's nose, he's making me violent just looking at him and I'm not a violent person, so get here before I do something I might end up getting in a lot of trouble for, please, Ben.'*

Ben stood up, and Morgan shrugged. 'I can handle the death message, you know that. You go sign the paperwork and then I can always meet you if the first address isn't the right one and you can come to the second one with me.'

He brushed past her, bending down to kiss the top of her head.

'I'm worried about Amy.'

'Why aren't we doing a cell site analysis for her phone by the way?'

This time Ben slapped his forehead. 'Christ, what's wrong with me. Yes, request one now, please, and hopefully the results will be back by the time I've been back to the scene.'

'I think we're panicking about everything. Deep breaths, Ben. Are you okay to drive? You looked a little bit peaky earlier.'

'I'm good, I'm never drinking neat whisky on a work night again. Please remind me of that the next time I think it's a good idea.'

He left her staring after him. Picking up the piece of paper she'd scribbled the addresses down on, she followed him out of the station and decided to drive to the Rydal Falls address first.

FORTY-THREE

Amy stared at the knife; it was taunting her, glinting on top of the drawers, but she couldn't get to it. She had been working at the pieces of material he'd used to bind her wrists for hours and her skin was red raw and painful. If she could slacken them enough to untie her feet she could grab the knife. He had left it there, taunting her with the unspoken threat that should she cause him any trouble he wouldn't hesitate to use it on her.

Anger wasn't even the right word to describe the boiling blackness that was raging inside of her, it was far more than that. Fear had numbed everything at finding herself in a situation like this – it was just incomprehensible. For God's sake, she'd been walking back to Cain's house, on her way to stop off at the estate agents and see if any affordable flats had just come onto the market. She thought about Morgan, who had got into all sorts of scrapes and survived, although it had been close a couple of times, but she did it. She survived and the only way to survive was to not give in. When she got free, she was going to beat the shit out of the guy who had done this to her. She didn't care about her job, her sanity or anything except putting him through the misery she'd been in for what? She looked at the old neon pink clock on the wall, over twenty-four hours. He'd brought her food and insisted she could only pee every four hours; it was agony holding it in because the more she thought about it the more she needed to go. She didn't know how long he was going to keep her captive like this before he did something that she might not survive. Her neck was so painful. He'd punched her or hit her with something, and she could barely turn to her right without a sharp pain shooting through her.

Noise on the landing made her entire body stiffen. He had been in here two hours ago, and he wasn't due for another two. All night he had kept to the four-hour rule as he'd called it. The heartburn she'd suffered from since the day she'd found out she was pregnant was burning the back of her throat almost as much as the skin on her wrists. The only thing she could do was to use the bucket he let her pee in. Throwing the hot liquid in his face then smashing him in the head with it so she could get to that blasted knife. Her head was much clearer now than when she'd first woken up in this floral explosion of the eighties. From the wallpaper and matching curtains to the bedding, everything was coordinated. If she stared at the tiny, pink rosebuds too long her eyes began to play tricks on her and they'd all start dancing, merging.

There was lots of movement outside, but he hadn't come in yet thankfully. Being held captive was making her weary too, or was it that injury to her neck? Either way she didn't think she'd be able to nap whilst tied to an armchair in a psychotic guy's bedroom, yet here she was, living out her worst nightmare and drifting off to sleep with exhaustion. She wondered if it was the fear that was making her body this tired. Helping her by making her sleep more than she ever did at home. Home, her life had been a nightmare the last six months. She had thought she and Jack would eventually get married, have kids, live to a ripe old age and grow old together. How wrong she'd been. Which proved just how crap a judge of character she was. Jack's reaction to her pregnancy had thrown her in a way she'd never realised could happen to her. Tough, angry, hard-working Amy had turned into a sobbing mess when he'd told her to get an abortion.

She closed her eyes. She thought that she would want to do that herself, kids had not been on either of their agendas for at least five years, according to Jack's plan. She struggled to understand his visceral reaction to the news he was going to be a dad. It still made her sad that she'd agreed to an abortion at first; so shocked by his reaction she had said anything to calm him down, telling herself it wasn't the right time. Then she'd thought about it, and it had been all she could think about, that tiny life growing inside of her, and she'd realised that she'd rather be on her own without Jack in her life as long as she had this baby to take care of.

Amy didn't realise she was crying until she felt the dampness trickling down her cheeks and neck, unable to lift her hands to blot away the tears.

The only person who had stood by her had been Cain, big, goofy, loud-mouthed Cain who had stepped up and offered her the support that Jack should have. He'd given her a home, a safe space to be whilst she figured things out. He'd talked to her for hours, into the early hours of the mornings, suggesting awful baby names that had made her laugh. Brought her pregnancy magazines and chocolates home every time he went shopping, and she realised she loved him more than any other man in her life.

She was happy Cain was happy with Angela, but she wished she'd realised how much of a match they were before he'd met Angela. She would never, ever do anything to jeopardise their relationship, but how she envied Angela, and although she complained and grouched about him, saying he was not being her birthing partner for a million quid, if she survived this then she would tell him she was sorry for being so mean, sorry for not realising what a great guy he was and that she would be honoured for him to be there when her baby was born. She couldn't think of a more suitable father figure than Cain Robson.

She began to twist her wrists and rub them even harder. She was not going to die or let her baby die before she'd even had the chance to be born. Amy was going to do what she could and fight for both of their lives. Before, she'd never thought about having a reason to live, but she bloody well had one now.

The door slammed open, and his dark shadow stood in the doorway, then he stepped into the room and shut it behind him.

FORTY-FOUR

Cain was crawling up and down the streets around his house, looking for Amy in case she'd been somewhere and was on her way home. His fingers clenching the steering wheel so hard he worried it might snap in two and then he'd be in trouble, but he was beyond worried. He didn't think Amy was the kind of woman to take her own life, but she wouldn't be the first. Look at Ben's wife Cindy, she had never suffered with depression, never cried for help, had on the outside lived a relatively happy, comfortable life with Ben. He had been first on scene that terrible night when Ben had phoned up screaming for someone to help his wife. He'd had to pull Ben out of the bathroom, Cindy's lifeless body on the floor, an empty vodka bottle next to her. Ben had been trying CPR to bring her back, but it was hopeless – by the time Ben had got home from working late she'd been dead a couple of hours.

Cain shuddered, he didn't know how Ben had coped with the grief. Amy wasn't his partner; they had never kissed, not even when drunk at the Christmas party, but he loved her. She was the closest thing he had to having children, and she was an almighty pain in the arse, but she was also his best friend. They had got really close since she'd moved in, and he felt fiercely protective over her and her baby. Now he was worried sick that something had happened to her, and he didn't know what or how he'd cope with any sort of tragic news. His phone broke his downward spiral of blackness that he'd been falling into.

'Robson.'

'It's Control, we have a hit on Amy's phone. Morgan requested a cell site analysis, and it's pinged off the masts near to Rydal Falls, Under Loughrigg road and...'

Cain felt his entire body erupt in goosebumps and he shivered. 'Under Loughrigg. Get patrols travelling to that area now. I'm on my way.'

'What location?'

'Under Loughrigg and all the surrounding areas, get them checking all the properties along the road.'

He hung up, dialling Ben's number. 'Boss, where are you?'

'At the woods, signing the paperwork for the body to be removed.'

Cain tried to keep his voice normal, but he knew it was close to breaking and it came out as a whisper. 'Amy's phone, it last connected to a mast between Rydal Falls and Under Loughrigg. She was walking, Ben, she wasn't in a car and the bodies were...' He did his best not to, but his voice broke, and he struggled to finish his sentence.

'I'm on my way, Cain, it's okay, we'll find her.'

But Cain wasn't so sure they were going to find her alive, that area was where the last two bodies had been likely thrown into the river and ended up caught up in Covel Woods. He had never felt so broken in his entire life as he sped to where he'd gone searching for the place the killer had parked to unload the bodies.

He screeched to a halt after a couple of close calls with some escaped sheep and a farmer trying to round them up. Normally he'd stop and help, sheep herding was one of his specialities, the amount of calls he'd attended whilst on patrol. He waved at the farmer as the window slid down. He asked. 'Have you seen a woman down here with reddish hair?'

The farmer looked at him and shook his head.

'A brown car maybe with her in the passenger seat?'

'Can't say I have.'

'Thanks.' He sped off. A lot could happen in twenty-four hours, hell he knew better than anyone that life could change in seconds, not hours, and he tried to keep the panic inside of his chest wedged down enough that he could still breathe.

FORTY-FIVE

Morgan had knocked loudly a couple of times on the semi-detached house. It looked as if it could do with a bit of loving to bring it back to its former glory. She walked to the gate, wondering if this was the house Mrs Decker lived in. If she lived alone there wasn't going to be any answer. They may have to put the door in if Theo confirmed this was her address; unless he could find someone with a key. Hopefully one of the neighbours would have a spare. As she pulled the gate shut, she glanced up at the window and saw a shadow step back. She watched to see if there was any more movement and decided to give one last knock in case whoever was up there was hard of hearing. Surely, they'd seen her at the gate. Knocking even harder she waited and was surprised to see the door open, but not as surprised as she was to see Gordon standing there with damp hair and looking a little red-faced.

'Oh, hey, Gordon. I didn't think anyone was in.'

'I was in the shower, I never heard you knocking, Morgan.'

'Do you live here?' She realised it was a stupid question as soon as the words left her mouth; he wouldn't be having a shower in a stranger's house, would he? Not unless he and Mrs Decker were good friends.

'I'm staying here whilst I'm covering for Theo.'

'Oh, can I come in?'

He looked as if he was going to say no. His eyes darting up and down the street, he opened the door, and she followed him inside. There was a strong chemical smell of ammonia lingering in the air. He led her into the kitchen and pointed to a chair, and she sat down but he stayed standing.

'I'm sorry, Morgan, it's been a day. What's up, you look very serious, I hope you haven't got some bad news for me?'

'We have a Mrs Decker listed as living here, is that correct?'

He nodded. 'Yes, that's right. I rent the house off her. Would you like a tea, coffee, glass of water?'

'I'm okay thanks. Do you know where she is at the moment?'

'I'm afraid not, I have no idea where Bertha is living to be honest. It's not something I've ever asked her; it doesn't seem right.'

At the mention of the name Bertha, Morgan felt every hair on the back of her neck prickle and a feeling of dread settled over her. She smiled at him, taking in the position where Gordon was standing. He had his back to the worktop but to the side of him was a knife block, a very full knife block, with only one empty space. All of them had shiny, stainless-steel handles and she imagined they were all very sharp. Bertha wasn't, as far as she knew, a popular name; in fact, she'd heard it for the first time in a long time when she'd read the statement from Aria Burns's neighbour who'd heard a woman's voice calling out for Bertha.

Gordon was looking more uncomfortable by the second. She needed to do something to distract him. 'Would you have a phone number for Bertha?' At this point she couldn't be sure Gordon was involved, but she wasn't giving anything away.

'Somewhere, let me check.'

He left the room to go into a room further down the hall-way, and it was then that she noticed the door next to the fridge. Did that lead to a garage or a cellar? Unable to stop herself she went to it and pushed the handle. It swung open, automatic lights turned on, and she felt her feet freeze to the spot at the sight of the two huge chest freezers with padlocks.

'What are you doing, Morgan?'

His voice was so close to her she felt his warm breath on the back of her neck, and she jumped. 'I'm sorry, I was looking for the loo and hoping this was a downstairs toilet.' She pulled the door shut and smiled at him. 'Sorry, I'm desperate.'

Gordon shook his head. 'What is it with you women and needing to pee so much? I'm glad us men don't need to go that often, it must be quite time consuming. I'd let you use the bath-room, but it's a mess. Like I said I've just got out of the shower. Here you are.'

He passed a Post-it note to her with a phone number scrib-bled onto it. 'You didn't tell me why you needed to speak to Bertha so urgently, I hope everything is okay.'

At that moment a loud thud from upstairs made the both of them look up.

'Who's up there?'

Gordon straightened up. 'It's probably Bertha's cat; she asked me to take care of it whilst she went away.'

'What kind of cat is it? A leopard, that was a loud thud.'

Gordon laughed. 'It's a big fat thing that doesn't move a lot. A bit like me to be fair.'

'I have a cat; he's always jumping off the furniture and going on the beds when he's not supposed to.'

She had to get upstairs, she had no handcuffs on her or CS gas, but she could grab a knife. Or she could walk out of the door and let him think she'd believed him. But if that was Amy up there, she might have just signed her death warrant. She took out her phone, deciding to ring Ben or Cain and tell them where she was before leaving and then watching the house from the outside. But before she could touch the keypad Gordon picked up a knife and pointed it at her.

'Give me the phone.'

'Why? What are you doing, Gordon, put the knife down.'

'I can't, why did you come here looking for Mrs Decker? The truth.' He jabbed the knife so close to her neck she felt the whoosh of air as the tip of it kissed her skin.

'I came looking for her family to pass on a death message.'

He tilted his head a little. 'You are good and this pains me greatly. I thought this would be over with before now. I thought that after my little hiccup yesterday with your friend, I had ruined things, then when nobody came looking, I realised that maybe I hadn't. Yet here you are. I really, really don't want to hurt you, Morgan.'

'Then let me walk out of here as if this didn't happen. I won't say anything.' Morgan couldn't help but think of Amy and her poor unborn child upstairs. 'You can get in your car and drive away; I'll give you enough time to get out of Cumbria before I call it in.'

'Call what in?'

'That you're a killer who's escaped my custody.'

He smiled at her. 'Very good, you are very astute, and this is why I like you. I don't believe you would be able to do that though. I think you would call it in the minute I left the house and this, I'm afraid to say, is the reason I must kill you.'

He lunged for her, and she managed to dive to one side. As he drew the knife back a second time, she caught movement out of the corner of her eye and pretended to slip, falling to the floor. Then he was standing above her, the knife raised high enough that when he thrust it towards her it would seriously injure if not kill her. But the knife clattered to the ground. The blade sliced her forearm as it bounced off it and a dazed Gordon stumbled forwards. He opened his mouth to speak and a bubble of blood burst out of it. Amy was standing behind him with bare feet, holding the missing knife from the block, its blade covered in bright red dripping blood. Gordon, unable to take any air into his lungs, looked like a fish out of water. Morgan realised Amy had punctured his lung as he fell forwards, gasping. She managed to roll out of his way before he landed on top of her, and she scrambled to her feet. Amy, who looked dishevelled, hugged her and Morgan hugged her back. She grabbed her phone and rang 999 then she rang Ben. Blood was seeping out of the deep wound in Gordon's back, and she turned to Amy.

'Are you okay?'

Amy nodded. 'I think so.'

'Put the knife on the table, Amy, I have to help him.'

Amy shook her head. 'No, you don't.'

'Yes, I do. We want him to go to court for this, not get out of it this way.'

Morgan grabbed a dry tea towel off the cooker door handle and rolled Gordon onto his side. Rolling the towel into a ball she pressed it as hard as she could against the hole in his back where the blood was seeping out and waited for paramedics and officers to come and relieve her. Amy sat down in a chair, her eyes glazed with shock but at least she was okay, and Morgan smiled at her. 'You did great.'

'I did.'

'Yes, you did.'

'Doesn't feel like it; at least you're not the one on the floor bleeding to death this time.'

Morgan shook her head; relieved Amy still had her sense of humour.

'No, it certainly makes a change.'

Sirens in the street got louder and louder, and Amy pushed herself up, hurrying to the front door to let the officers inside. Within a matter of minutes, the house was full of uniformed officer, paramedics, and then Cain came rushing through the door followed by Ben. She had let the paramedics take over on Gordon. Cain had Amy wrapped in his arms, and Ben pointed to the cut on Morgan's arm. 'What the hell happened here?'

She pointed to Gordon. 'Someone better read him his rights.'

Cain smiled at her. 'Well, well, Brookes, look at you. One job, you had one job to deliver a death message, but you couldn't even do that without causing total mayhem. Well done, though. I mean seriously well done.'

Ben had picked up another towel and was wrapping it around the gash in her arm.

'We better get you to the hospital. You too, Amy. You need a check-up to make sure everything is okay.'

Amy didn't argue with them. 'I'll go if Cain can take me, but I got to pee first.'

Morgan smiled at her. 'That's what Gordon meant when he said us women always need to pee.'

When Amy was ready, Cain took her out to the car, and Morgan waited until they were driving away before she spoke to Ben. Gordon was being placed onto a stretcher to be whisked away to hospital.

'I'm so sad it was Gordon. I never in a million years expected that when he opened the door, but it all makes sense. Theo said Gordon mentored him and I didn't think much of it at the time, but the only other church Theo worked in was Birmingham. Gordon must have killed Martha MacKay and kept her body. I don't know why he killed Mrs Decker though?'

'We'll see what turns up when the house is searched, there must be some connection if this is her house.'

'I have an idea I know where Aria Burns might be.'

'You do?'

She pointed to the garage door and, seeing as how she'd already touched it and her fingerprints were all over it, she pulled it open, waiting for the lights to blink on. When they did, Ben let out a small, 'Holy crap,' at the sight of the freezers.

She pointed to them. 'I think Aria is inside one of those. Can we take a look and check? I need to know.'

Pulling gloves out of his pocket, he tugged them onto his hands. 'You know Wendy is going to kill the pair of us, but you're right. We need to check before we seal the house off.'

She followed him to the freezer, holding the towel around her arm tightly so the blood didn't drip onto the floor and contaminate the scene any further. Both freezers had padlocks on them, but they hadn't been snapped shut. Ben slipped the first one off and lifted the lid, as Morgan held her breath. It was empty, and she let out a sigh of relief. He moved across to the second one and did the same. As he lifted the lid Morgan let out a small gasp of horror. There was a face staring up at them, ice crystals dusting her thick black eyelashes. Morgan had never actually expected to find a body. But it wasn't Aria who was frozen in time, she was or had been a beautiful Asian girl.

Morgan felt an overwhelming sadness fill her soul as she leaned forward and whispered, 'Hello, I don't know your name yet, but I will and, as soon as we do, I'm going take you home.'

Tears flowed down her cheeks at the sight of the beautiful young woman forever frozen in time, and she didn't try to stop them, she couldn't if she wanted to – the horror and injustice was too much even for Morgan to comprehend. She was crying for whoever this was and for Aria. She had expected to find her but now she thought that may not be likely, maybe Gordon had nothing to do with her disappearance after all.

'Well, would you look at this. Why am I not surprised to see you two here, bawling all over my crime scene, adding insult to injury.'

Both jumped at the sound of Wendy's voice as it echoed around the garage.

'Get the fuck out of here before I call the cops.' They

turned to look at her, but she winked at them. 'Good job, Morgan, supercop does it again and with only a minor injury to show for it. You must be getting better at this job.'

Morgan smiled at her. 'Thanks, nobody is more surprised than I am.'

They squeezed past Wendy.

'I bet they're not. Tell me, Morgan, is any of that yours?' She was pointing to the pool of blood on the kitchen floor.

'Not this time, at least I don't think so.'

'I hope not, last thing I need is you giving my scene a little extra contamination for old times' sake.'

Ben grabbed Morgan's hand. 'Come on, let's get you out of here. This is going to take some time to process.'

She wasn't about to argue with him over that. Reaching the doorway she stopped as a muffled thump came from behind the freezer. Morgan turned back slowly.

'Did you hear that?'

Everyone shook their heads and continued talking. She lifted a finger to her lips, shushing them loudly as another, almost barely audible, bang came from the wall again. She pointed to the freezer with the body in and rushed back.

'Help me move this.'

Wendy snapped some quick photos before rushing with Ben and Cain to drag it away from the wall. It was heavy, and both Morgan and Wendy grunted as they managed to pull it away.

'Give me your torch.' Morgan held out the palm of her hand towards Wendy, and she passed her powerful torch to her. Switching it on, she crouched down and saw what looked like a garden gate that had been bolted across a hole in the wall.

All of them stared at it until it juddered as another thump came from behind it.

Wendy passed Morgan and Ben some gloves, the whole time filming on her body camera as the pair of them crouched down and began to work loose the six bolts that had been fitted each below the other. As Morgan pushed back the final bolt she sucked in her breath, a little afraid of what they were going to find behind the gate.

It swung open and she directed the beam of light inside a blackness so consuming it was hard to see anything until the light reflected off a pair of eyes. Morgan jumped and realised that she knew those dark brown eyes. She'd studied them long enough.

'Aria?'

The girl who looked terrified stared back at her.

'It's okay, you're safe now. I'm a police officer.'

Morgan held out her hand and there was a scrabbling sound as Aria crawled towards her, the sound of chains dragging on the floor. She saw that her feet were chained up to the wall.

'Get me some bolt cutters now,' she shouted at everyone, hoping that someone had a pair in the van.

Morgan crawled inside of the cramped space, her torchlight picking out a mattress and an orange bucket. Her nose wrinkled. It smelled bad inside but she crawled towards Aria, opening her arms. The young woman fell into them, her entire body shaking as she cried and sobbed into Morgan's shoulder. Morgan held her tight, gently rocking her from side to side until someone could come and cut the chains off her ankles and set her free.

Morgan whispered, 'I'm taking you home, sweetheart, everything is going to be okay now.'

Aria held tight onto her and wouldn't let go, not even when Ben crawled in with the bolt cutters. She flinched away from him, a high-pitched keening sound coming from her lips.

'It's okay, this is my partner, Ben, he's a police officer too. He's going to cut those chains off your feet. He won't hurt you, I promise. Do you trust me?'

Aria nodded, then held still so he could cut her free. He

backed out first, then Morgan, who waited patiently for Aria to come out, but the woman was reluctant to move. Morgan held out her hands towards her.

'You're safe, I promise that he can't hurt you ever again. He's on his way to the hospital. One of my colleagues stabbed him. It's his turn to be locked up in a cell for the rest of his life.'

Aria's shoulders dropped at this point, and she placed her hands in the prayer position before finally crawling towards Morgan, who helped her out.

Ben slammed the lid of the freezer shut before she stood up and saw the body inside of it. Morgan knew they had a lot of work to do to identify the dead woman and get her back to her parents, so they could finally bury the daughter they had been missing for far too long. Hers was not a happy ending, but at least Aria's parents would get their daughter back. God knows how she would get over the trauma of what Gordon had put her through, but she was alive and that was a start.

As Morgan led Aria out of the house to waiting paramedics, all the officers, including Wendy, Cain, Ben and Marc who had arrived, began to clap and not a single person had a dry eye. This was more than Morgan could ever have hoped for. That Aria had been found meant more to her than anything and she was glad to have been the one to do just that. Her job was tough, heartbreaking and tiring but she would never stop fighting criminals, because good always overcame evil in the end, and Morgan was happy she was the one who got to do that, to bring them to justice and hopefully bring a little bit of peace to the many grieving families who had suffered so much.

EPILOGUE

Morgan felt bad for Theo. When they had broken the news to him, he had cried big, heartfelt wracking sobs. It wasn't just about Gordon; it was everything that had happened in the last few months. She held him tight, rocking him gently – she was getting better at this hugging thing. She had never been a hugger, but that was before when she didn't have anyone to care enough about to hug. Theo took in a deep breath and sighed. She passed him a wad of tissues out of the box on the table, and he dabbed at his eyes.

'Sorry, Morgan, I feel like such a fool but it's this, the whole shock of everything... and Gordon—' He stopped talking, inhaled deeply then exhaled a slow, long breath before continuing. 'Gordon is such a nice man; I cannot comprehend any of this. I am gutted that he has hurt those girls like he has. I haven't slept since he was arrested, as it keeps going over and over in my head why he would do this.'

'I know, I feel so betrayed. I really liked him too. I suppose he carried that darkness around inside of himself, and tried to keep it under control by being a priest, but it won, didn't it?'

Theo nodded. 'I've never been in a police station to hear a confession before. Do you think he's doing it to brag?'

She shook her head. 'No, I think he wants to tell his side of the story and get it over with, and I think that he likes you enough for you to want to hear it first-hand. He insisted in the hospital that when he was interviewed, he would give a full confession if you were there, and me.'

Ben walked into the room with a clipboard and paused. 'Do you need a moment?'

Theo looked at him. 'No, I'm good. Sorry for being so foolish.'

Ben clamped a hand on Theo's shoulder and gently squeezed. 'You're not being foolish, this is just another day for us, it's what we do. Day in, day out, don't worry about it. Are you both ready?'

They nodded. 'Good, then I'll tell his solicitor.'

The Gordon who was led into the room in handcuffs was a shadow of his former self, his face ashen and gaunt. He'd been in hospital for ten days, then discharged and brought straight here. He didn't make eye contact with any of them as he sat down; he kept his gaze downcast.

Ben spoke, introducing each person by name for the camera that was recording in the corner of the room.

'Gordon, are you ready to talk?'

He nodded then looked straight at Morgan. 'How's your arm, Morgan?'

She rolled up her sleeve to show him the row of stitches. 'It's good, almost mended.'

Gordon turned to Theo. 'How are you, Theo?'

Theo looked at Ben who nodded. 'I'm not that good if I'm honest, Gordon.'

'No, I suppose this was all a bit of a shock for you.'

'Yes. How are you?'

A sly smile crossed Gordon's lips for a moment before his face was serious again.

'I'm in a bit of a mess, but you know that, my friend. I don't need to explain why to you, or we wouldn't be sitting here like this. It's nice though, I'm glad they let you come in. I feel as if I need to confess my sins to God this once so I can move on.'

Morgan was watching Gordon intently. He wasn't anything like the friendly, funny vicar she thought she had known, and it shocked her to the core. This was a different version of the Gordon they all knew, and she wondered which one was the real Gordon: the sweet, kind, funny vicar or the mean, cold, evil killer.

'I am ready to confess my sins, are you ready to hear them?'

They nodded.

'I took Martha MacKay the night she was sheltering from the cold. I asked her for a sexual favour and led her out of the church to the canal. I can't say why exactly it happened, but I knew I didn't want to have sex with her. I wanted to kill her; this urge I have now and again up until that point had been kept under control. At that point it took over everything and before I knew it, I was holding up her lifeless body and panicked; only she wasn't dead, and I decided to take her home with me. I must have caused serious damage to her nervous system though because she couldn't move or speak when she did open her eyes. I kept her for a little while, unsure why, but then I realised that you wouldn't keep a dog in that state, so I did what was best and hit her again on the side of the neck, only this time much harder.'

Gordon stopped and licked his dry, chapped lips before reaching for the plastic cup of water on the table. He took a couple of sips, coughed to clear his throat.

'I tried to kill Aria Burns, the night she went missing. I met her in the playing fields and well, she didn't die either. She was still alive and she was far too pretty to kill, so I made her a little home away from home in the cellar, and I suppose you know the rest. Oh, actually, did you find her there or did you miss her little abode?' He licked his lips again, a grin stretching his lips back into some grotesque caricature of his former self.

'That would be a terrible shame, as her food and water would have run out by now. I imagine she's quite dead after all.'

Ben smiled at him. 'Actually, Aria is as well as she can be thanks to Morgan discovering the room you kept her chained up in like some wild animal.'

Gordon looked mildly annoyed at this news and paused before continuing.

'I took her home and the next day I travelled to Manchester to find another girl to put in one of the freezers I'd bought, to keep Martha company. I knew nothing about her. I snatched her off the street. She was very drunk and it was very late. She didn't put up a fight. I think she'd had enough of life anyway, so I did her a favour.' He sighed. 'The pair of them were more beautiful in death than they'd ever been in life. They were my ice angels, and I spent much time staring at them. Of course, keeping that girl alive was more trouble than it was worth. She was hard to control, but luckily for me by the time she came around I had already bound her hands and feet and gagged her so she couldn't make much sound. That little home I made I hadn't intended to actually use, but it did come in handy. I had thought long and hard about putting my mother inside of there, but I never got around to that.'

Morgan couldn't stop watching Gordon, the way his tongue kept feeling his teeth, licking at his lips.

Ben asked. 'Why did you kill Mrs Decker?'

Gordon threw back his head and laughed. It was loud, and it seemed to take forever for him to get control of himself.

Theo couldn't help it. 'Was it because of that awful calendar idea she came up with?'

'I'd like to say it was, Theo, but that was only a little part of the problem with Bertha Decker.'

'What problem?' asked Ben.

'Bertha Decker was the worst mother anyone could have asked for. I never asked for her yet that's what I got. She was cruel, she disowned me a long time ago, but then she got ill and needed someone to run around after her. She had been begging my forgiveness for years, especially when she found out that her pathetic, weak son had become a vicar. She called and pleaded with me to come home; and then I was asked to cover for Theo whilst he recovered from that awful attack which was so uncalled for. I thought that I could kill two birds with one stone, so I did. I went home and it was the worst mistake I ever made. I made her promise not to acknowledge me as her son at church. To be quite frank with you, I didn't want anything to do with her and the longer I lived with her the more I knew she had to go.'

'You didn't want to keep her preserved like the others, why was that?'

'I was not having Bertha Decker contaminate my beautiful ice angels. I wanted to drag her into that dark hole and lock her in like she did to me when I was a boy, but I didn't have the courage to do it to her, until I finally found the courage to kill her instead.'

'Can you explain your reasoning behind abducting Amy Smith?'

'Pure greed, the opportunity arose, and I pounced on it without thinking about the finer details. It was problematic when I realised she was pregnant. I'm a monster, but I have some morals, and it was a real dilemma for me deciding if she should live or die.'

Morgan glanced at the two-way mirror she knew Cain and Amy were standing behind, listening in. She asked, 'Why did you put Martha in the river?'

His eyes fell on Morgan's, and he stared at her. 'I needed to make some room; I had managed after Aria to reel the darkness back inside. I knew I'd made a mistake, and I had to keep a low profile which is another reason I came to live with my mother. I had to leave Birmingham, and it was the perfect excuse.'

It was Ben's turn to ask Gordon questions. 'Why did you need to make more room?'

He smiled at him, but his gaze fixed on Morgan. 'I wanted to add you to my collection, Morgan, why do you think?'

She saw Ben's fingers clench hard and reached out a hand underneath the table. She gently squeezed his fist, and he breathed out the air he'd sucked in and had been holding.

'Yes, you would have made an exquisite addition to my collection, although I screwed everything up by taking Amy instead. She was, I suppose, the next best thing. I had to finally do something about my awful mother when she opened the freezer and saw the girl. It's such a good job I came home and caught her in the act; I finally did what I'd dreamed about for all those years. I killed her; a fast, precise well-aimed blow to the side of the neck is all you need to knock someone out. Hit them hard enough and you can kill them, which is what happened to Martha the second time. I was a martial arts teacher for years before I joined the priesthood.'

Gordon turned to Theo. 'Forgive me, Father, for I have sinned.' And then he began to laugh, uncontrollable laughter that filled the room as he started rocking back and forth in his chair.

Ben ended the interview and made everyone leave except the police officer who was standing behind Gordon, his hand on his taser.

As they walked out of the room, Gordon began to scream. 'The devil made me do this, he's here right now and he's watching all of you. He wants you for himself. You're no better than I am. He's biding his time and then when you least expect it, he'll be there, whispering over your shoulder and you might not be able to rebuke him. Let him in, he'll show you a wild ride.'

It had been decided that Gordon wasn't going to a prison, at least not until they could prove he was faking this mental illness that had come on swiftly; he was going to a secure psychiatric hospital because of his behaviour. He'd been laughing uncontrollably for over an hour now and had threatened to kill himself multiple times. His solicitor had advised that he be assessed on the grounds of his mental health.

Marc, who had been watching along with Amy and Cain, had agreed and they were now waiting for him to be transferred. Oh the irony, thought Morgan. She had been talking about where Ian Brady had been detained and now Gordon would shortly be on his way to Ashworth Hospital in Liverpool.

Declan had been waiting the whole time in a small room with a sofa and box of toys they kept for anyone who'd been detained with children, and he stood up and hugged Theo when Morgan brought him to him; and then Theo walked out of the station to the car with his hand in Declan's, and out of Gordon's life.

———

Marc ushered them all back into the office and announced, 'I'm going for coffee, be right back.'

Cain arched an eyebrow at them all and waited for him to leave the room before he said, 'Amy, I think he might have let you live, but you' – he pointed a finger at Morgan – 'you were definitely going to end up in one of those freezers.'

'Cain,' both Amy and Morgan said at the same time.

'What? I'm just stating the obvious. It's a good job you accidentally caught him, or we'd be defrosting your body now like a Christmas turkey.'

'Cain,' Ben warned him, and he shrugged.

'At least the boss is buying the coffees. Come on, why are you all looking so sad? Morgan, you did good, you're both alive. We should have an *I didn't die party* for you both instead of a baby shower.'

Amy stood up, walked around behind him and clamped a hand over his mouth.

'If you don't shut up, we'll put you in a freezer.'

He held up his hands. 'Sorry, I didn't realise you'd lost your sense of humour.'

Morgan grinned at the pair of them.

Amy was now hugging Cain from behind and he was beaming. He nodded in Amy's direction. 'See, she loves me really.'

As sad and horrifying as this all was, Morgan was glad she had her little work family to keep her sane.

Ben, who had disappeared into his office, came out with a sheet of paper and passed it to her.

'I realised that you never booked that holiday. We're flying to Boston in five days and then on to Salem for a week before flying to New York for four nights.'

Morgan squealed with delight. 'Really?'

'Yes, really. I am sick of sharing you with these idiots. It's time to have you all to myself.'

She hugged him then, not caring that Amy and Cain were watching, not caring that she'd almost been Gordon's next victim. Life was good at times as long as you didn't let the bad times get you down. There was always something brighter on the horizon and she knew that better than anyone.

A LETTER FROM HELEN

I want to say a huge thank you for choosing to read *Twisted Bones*. If you did enjoy it, and want to keep up-to-date with all my latest releases, just sign up at the following link. Your email address will never be shared and you can unsubscribe at any time.

www.bookouture.com/helen-phifer

I hope you've enjoyed Morgan's, Ben's, Cain's, Marc's, Wendy's and poor Amy's adventure. You'll see I listened, Morgan's head has been given a well-deserved rest and she only got a cut on her arm this time, which I'm pretty sure she would have stuck a plaster on if Ben hadn't insisted she get it looked at. I honestly can't thank you enough for reading these books that I write. Spending time with Morgan and her team is like having a catch-up with a group of my best friends. They are lots of fun, cause me to laugh a lot and worry about them too. I get a knot in my stomach at what I'm putting them through as I write it, but what a glorious job.

I dreamed about becoming a full-time author one day, when I was working full-time shifts as a police community support officer and writing in my spare time. Because of you, my wonderful readers, I was able to make that dream my reality three years ago. It meant that I could write around being able to spend time with my family who are my whole world. Looking after my son Jaimea who has many additional needs and disabilities can be very challenging at times, and writing for me is a way to leave my world and live in another for a short time. It's nice to be in control of my fictional world because sometimes my own is utter chaos, but I wouldn't have it any other way and I'm so thankful to you all for making this possible.

I hope you loved *Twisted Bones* and if you did I would be very grateful if you could write a review. I'd love to hear what you think, and it makes such a difference helping new readers to discover one of my books for the first time.

I love hearing from my readers – you can get in touch on my social media or my website.

Thanks,

Helen

www.helenphifer.com

facebook.com/Helenphifer1
x.com/helenphifer1

ACKNOWLEDGEMENTS

Where do I start? There are so many people it takes to turn a first draft into the book you have just read.

The biggest thank you goes to my wonderful, lovely editor Jennifer Hunt. Her brilliant insights are what helps to make this story as good as it can be, and I love working with you so much, Jennifer, you really are the nicest person and I can't thank you enough.

Thanks also to the amazing team Bookouture who are just so fabulous and will have their own mentions on the next pages. I was shocked by just how many brilliant people there are who work on my stories and I'm very grateful to you all. A special mention to Jenny Geras for being a brilliant, inspirational woman, Kim Nash for always looking out for me, Noelle Holten for being my publicity wing gal and always having my back. Jan Currie for her amazing copy editing and Shirley Khan for her proofreading.

A heartfelt thank you to you, my amazing readers, for loving Morgan and Ben so much. I wouldn't be writing this at the end of book fifteen if it wasn't for you and I love you all. I hope you know how wonderful you are. Book people truly are the best people.

A special thank you to all the book bloggers and reviewers who so tirelessly spend their time reading and sharing their love of books with us all. How lucky we are to have you and I truly appreciate all of your support.

Thank you to the lovely Jess Sylvester Yeo who is my lifesaver when it comes to Instagram and TikTok content, you really are the loveliest person I could ask for to help me and I really appreciate everything you do.

I would not be able to write these books without the wonderful support that Selena, Dan and Jenny give to Jaimea. Your kindness and love mean the world to me, to know that Jaimea is so loved by you all fills my heart with so much joy. Thank you all, but especially Selena for everything you do.

A special thank you to the real-life Amy Smith whose name I stole in the early days, and for making Amy's character so feisty but loveable. Not only did I make you pregnant, I almost killed you, sorry. I promise no more drama for a while for you.

Another huge thank you to the amazing staff at Mill Lane Day Services, for helping to make Jaimea's life so full and for giving us all a chance to breathe and drink coffee through the day.

As always, a huge, heartfelt thank you to the amazing Paul O'Neill for casting his eye over this and his brilliant surveyor's reports. Honestly, Paul, you are my lifesaver.

Thank you to my beautiful family, for being so unique, amazing, fun, sometimes stressful. Jessica, I'm not mentioning your name at all, you didn't stress me out one bit whilst trying to finish this book 🙂

But I'm truly blessed to have these amazing souls in my life and a special thank you to Jerusha for being such a beautiful cheerleader and listening to me tell you about my writing life and what's going on in it. Jess, Josh, Jaimea, Jeorgia, Danielle, Deji, and Tom, I love you almost as much as I love your kids and thank you from the bottom of my heart for giving me such brilliant grandkids who make my life and my heart so happy. Gracie, Donny, Lolly, Tilda, Sonny, Shopping Queen Sie-Sie and dancing Queen Bonnie your nanna is so proud of you, and I couldn't love you anymore.

Lastly thank you to Steve, he's been in my life for the last thirty-seven years and the best bag carrier I could ask for.

Much love to everyone,

Helen xx

PUBLISHING TEAM

Turning a manuscript into a book requires the efforts of many people. The publishing team at Bookouture would like to acknowledge everyone who contributed to this publication.

Audio
Alba Proko
Sinead O'Connor
Melissa Tran

Commercial
Lauren Morrissette
Hannah Richmond
Imogen Allport

Cover design
The Brewster Project

Data and analysis
Mark Alder
Mohamed Bussuri

Editorial
Jennifer Hunt
Charlotte Hegley